DIRTMOUTH

DIRTMOUTH

ALAN SINGER

FC2
NORMAL/TALLAHASSEE

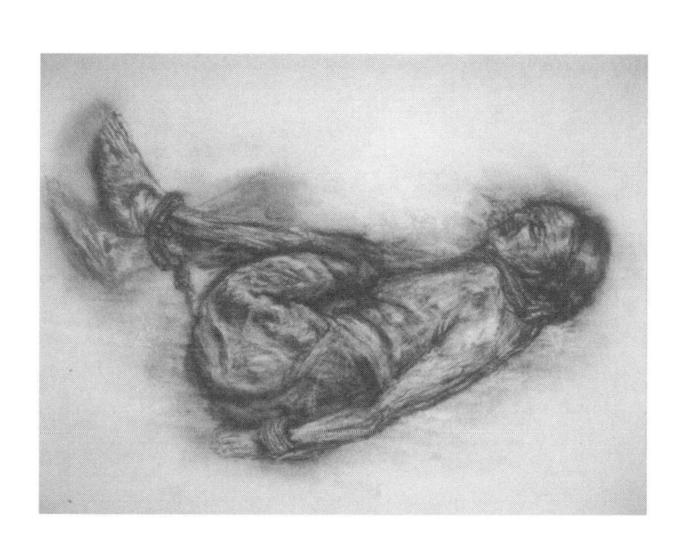

First Edition
First Printing 2004

Published by FC2 with support provided by Florida State University, the Publications Unit of the Department of English at Illinois State University, and the Illinois Arts Council.

Address all inquiries to: Fiction Collective Two, Florida State University, c/o English Department, Tallahassee, FL 32306-1580

ISBN: Paper, 1-57366-117-1

Library of Congress Cataloging-in-Publication Data
Singer, Alan, 1948-
Dirtmouth / by Alan Singer.— 1st ed.
p. cm.
ISBN 1-57366-117-1
1. Young women—Crimes against–Fiction. 2. Archaeologists—Fiction. I. Title.
PS3569.I526D57 2004
813'.54—dc22
2004004923

Cover Design: Lou Robinson
Original Drawings: Toni Serratelli
Book Design: Jeremy Coulter and Tara Reeser

Produced and printed in the United States of America.
Printed on recycled paper with soy ink.

OTHER NOVELS BY ALAN SINGER

The Ox-Breadth

The Charnel Imp

Memory Wax

ACKNOWLEDGMENTS

Excerpts of this novel appeared in:

TriQuarterly (Summer 2003), as "Bog Pastoral"

Western Humanities Review (Spring 2003), as "Find Site"

FOR NORA

Death is the mother of beauty, mystical,
Within whose burning bosom we devise
Our earthly mothers waiting, sleeplessly.

Wallace Stevens, “Sunday Morning”

PROLOGUE

I am here to listen to you listen to each other. The questions will be my own, the better to prise the difference between your stories.

I see you are fat. You are thin. You are old. You are young. You are bald. You are hirsute. But these are only my eyes talking, and using such simple words. The crime before us is something more complex. It wants another vision, because what we hunt for here is what the watering eye cannot make out unless it makes itself invisible.

And what if I didn't ask the questions? What if I were patient? What if we sat together and my lips were sealed? Only the ticking of the timepiece, knocking against the steady breath of our bodies at rest. Then would you hear the ghostly voices of my questions in spontaneous utterances that you yourselves might mount against the uncomfortable silence? Fidgeting in your uncomfortable chairs, would you become me by presuming upon my silence? Would you impersonate my questions? It could be that you would even forget yourselves in telling me what it is you think I want to hear. One of you might even confess. Shall we perform the experiment? Shall we?

Very well. Then I'll ask the questions.

You ask. So I will tell you the truth. Mind, it will take some time. I have already walked on this earth long enough that you may not have the patience to catch up with me. And that is not the end of my apologies.

I will talk. But I warn you. I cannot open my mouth without releasing an exhalation from the grave. Bad breath isn't a lick of it, doesn't begin to describe the sour vapors that will rise from what our young colleague sitting beside us might call my carcass.

I admit, bad breath is too animate. What I give off from my parted lips reposes more deeply in the buried earth of my physique. Without the undignified exhumation of my every spoken word, such moldering knowledge would remain as inert as the unscratched skin of an overripe cheese.

But the wax rind of my constitution is vastly pricked and scarred with the rough handling of eighty-three years on Blackman's Heath.

What I breathe out, even to say it—and so with more apologies—is the everlasting death of all the food that I have ever eaten. Look on my heaped belly and think of it. The fumes waft from the mortuary of my repasts. Worse yet, they are memorialized in what I now discover to be an ominous cellular accretion in the pit of my stomach. It communicates to my probing fingers a curious tenderness. No doubt the callous of a life's digestion.

Like the rings of a stately trunk or the linked chambers of a mollusk's whorled carapace, what I feel as a foreign body buried in my gut is, in fact, the only faculty of memory left to me, since memory, in this case, is no part of my mind. In this fingertip sensation there reposes the hard—and harder to contemplate—certainty that my body will survive me, if only to become food for more wriggling appetites: what is to come.

What better irony then, that I, an eighty-three-year-old Archeologist Emeritus, professor of the past, am a man without memory?

But the more startling irony by far is that because *here and now* I am incapable of remembering anything longer ago than the interval between mealtimes, I am endlessly a source of new life to myself. New life carried on the bier of physical decrepitude, moving forward against the tide of the funeral procession.

So I will seem to insist with that much more pathos than the average soul of senility, that there is a way in which the eighty-three-year-old codger is young. There is a way in which my failing memory is the flower of that youth. No. I am not the prisoner abandoned in the darkness of his fleshly dungeon, dismally lost to himself as well as to others.

I know what I am, because I know what I am becoming.

And it is thanks to the pathology of my forgetfulness that I am daily becoming something more than I was. As with all youthful endeavors, the exuberant evidence of this self-knowledge is that I am becoming a stranger to regrets. Without memory I am immune to loss. So if I am young, this immunity is the vigor of that youth. In these thoughts I am inoculated against the virulence of my bodily ache. And if the grave speaks through the vapors of my digested life, it augurs an unexpected gestation. These lips will suffer the distortions of a difficult labor.

They know not what they may come to say.

So *here and now* I sit in the docket, so to speak, the weight of everything that I have eaten, ready to say what I have done to the woman whom you laughingly call my *lover*. Because that is the question you have asked.

The answer is, I loved her.

But now you must challenge the answerability of your own question. Ask me how can a man without memory recollect even the most recent past without forgetting who he is in the act of telling it? Who is he to tell it? Of whom does he speak to tell it? You will notice that I do not use the word *remember*.

I ask you to think of the memory problem in terms of the body: its comings and goings. Mouth and anus. Lips that never touch though they are kissing cousins, and though the stomach puckers between them, a nervous pander to their wayward passions. Does the uncoiling stool remember the intestinal embrace? It is, of course, the wrong question.

It is not a question of memory but of growth. What one eats becomes one *without* one's knowing it. No past and present about it. The hand stroking the belly makes no real acquaintance with the fullness of a big meal. There are no cytoplasmic reckonings between the sensitive skin that gloves caressing fingers, and the abdomen shedding sensations of familiarity to make the body swell. My bigger self is someone else, to be met as a stranger, perhaps a lover.

So even growing old I am also growing. It is indeed more than fingernails and hair growing into perpetuity. Even you fear that I grow more than such a corpse would do. And it is much more than the heap of my middle. The hand that pats the belly full waves farewell to the appetite from which new heft has sprung. The knowledge of what hungers after the next hole in the belt loop has passed it by. Mere memory is no match for growth. Like an old man, thing of the past itself, memory is nothing but a shadow, the better to bring out the shine of the young man's youth.

So believe me. The one who speaks to you *here and now* is the one who is most present. I am the youthful moment of your question. And I augur the most momentous answer.

Let me shine!

Loved a man without memory? A body a corpse couldn't envy? A smell that crannies like a worm up your nose? I ask you.

You know she was a young woman. She had limbs that could bend. She had breasts. They stood up. You didn't have to bend your neck to nip them. I know. She had legs. They walked.

They ran. An old man like that would have burst a lung to keep pace.

Between her legs there pumped the heart of a champion runner breasting the tape. I was there at the end of the race. And no spectator, I assure you.

He is an old man. But I still say he is a killer.

If he thinks she loved him, it is an understandable misprision. The dulled sense infallibly mistakes what is with what it wishes for. What drew Cinna to his failing physique was only the scent of fatherhood that we all sniff to in a solitary hour. All dogs off the leash wander back to the master's footprints before they finally tear away. She had her wistfulness, but it was nothing that tied her.

And have you followed *his* footprints? Don't be fooled by the millstone girth he bemoans so loudly. It makes you think of him always in a chair. It makes you think of his backside, not his devious brain. Not only in a chair. I can tell you. He gets around. He has been around this heath forever, which you already know, and which is why each earth-shattering find harvested from this celebrated bog has left its imprint on the record book of his personal fame: *Archeologist Emeritus. Fellow of the Anthropological Institute.* Gilded character.

Let's see what a chip of gilt reveals.

No one ever asked how is it that he owned the heath *before* it became the deed-bearer of his good name. How was it the heir to the Blackman Estate ascended directly to head of this sovereign state of affairs, wielding all powers over the society of the dig? I am telling you, there are more questions to be answered here and now than you've yet scratched from your flaking scalp.

For example, how does a man who protests the purest innocence report the crime before he has any right to suspect a crime has been committed? He tells us frankly that, like every invalid, he lives in.

And how does he claim to know where the victim's body lies, who in the same breath confesses that he would not step outside the house, because at his age he fears the boggy ground beneath his feet? He protests it can no longer support the weight of his stride beyond the gated wall that rings the manor round. He trembles to say that wall is all that holds the house against the mire of sucking dampness. He wants us to think of him thinking that the wet ground waits without like the beast of devour. His feet are always slippered. Seldom booted anymore. He points it out at the tips of his toes. "I stay at home, right enough" he mumbles coyly to your mustachioed investigator. He says he must be carried in and out. There is his sedan chair.

Then why are his socks so wooly around his ankles? Why does the ruddiness in his cheeks look so fresh. How do the calluses grow upon such idle thumbs? And why are the steps to the library entrance encrusted with what can only be boot scrapings from the dankest sewers of mud?

His mind was always a shovel wasn't it? Why shouldn't his arms be able to shoulder it still? His whole fatty self would be the most efficient leverage against the most obstinate spadeful of peat.

And how could a body that would sink in the mud have floated on the translucent skin of her ardor? She was passionate, but she was frail. You could see the blood swimming under her skin where it dipped between her legs.

Let's not delude ourselves, with that belly he would have sunk to the bottom. She wouldn't have had the strength to dredge him up.

Ask yourself. Could she have loved a man with a body from which nothing will rise? The flesh only falls from it. I can tell you she made no fetish of gravity. He's a man you can sit next to and you feel yourself sinking into a mire. His breathing is a torpor of humidity. The asthmatic soughing of his lungs is a haze of mosquitoes over a fermenting scum. A lagoon, of a man in a bog of a country. Imagine the attraction!

Could she have loved a man like that? He told us himself! You can't imagine the body he keeps inside his clothes without thinking of ripening cheese. You wouldn't tamper with a loose flap of the yellowing cloth that clings to the cheese, like nothing so much as the damp sheath of cotton underwear in which his erect penis is furled. Think of the smell of it in her hand and ask if you can hold it even in your most gingerly thoughts of him. How flaccid is your revulsion in the instant of your knowing that what I say is true?

Why do we ask ourselves such questions? My answer to you here and now, is that *because* he is an old man, he is a killer. This is how we understand.

We need to know what we are up against. So I'll tell you: it is the wrath of decrepitude. Ire rejuvenates the slackest musculature. But even if the strength of arm can't be summoned to the deed, the mind is all the more willing and able. Isn't it? And haven't you noticed that it is the enfeebled mind, of which the professor does not cease to complain, that wants to persuade you of the greater incapacity of the body—which he says he drags around like a dead man? Can a corpse be the murderer, you want to ask.

It can be so if deadness is what it hates most: the fading ear, the nose evaporating into the odors that ought to make it shiver, the taste buds that must be flogged against one's food to raise a flavor like dust on a dry road. The deadening of the senses is the strongest incentive to snuff them out in another physique. The one who is dying yearns to be a more virulent form of the disease. And if he is only dying of years that is all the more reason to carry the weight of his body like a scythe against a brother or a sister. As I say, the vengeful mind would have been whetstone to that dull blade.

A passionate thought—and isn't vengeance the sweaty ardor of the mind?—has been known to fire a spurt of physical fortitude that surpasses the ordinary capacities of the most debilitated frame. How much stronger if the thought despises the body itself in its stumbling, stammering travesty of well being?

A spotty-faced, palsy-limbed eighty-three-year-old monster of decrepitude. He is. And she was twenty seven. No doubt he wanted her body. But not for his own. In place of his own. Parasite!

So don't ask whether he did it. Ask yourself: how?

My young colleague forgets the passionate peal of his own voice to speak of passion so cruelly. And he is wrong on two counts. First, passion ought never to be confused with anger. Anger is just the body's heat and none of its light. Second, here and now, I am ready to say that I had not been a passionate man—perhaps had never known passion—before I clothed her bones in my flesh. Yes, I was an angry man before Cinna loved me.

And I say again, she loved me, whomever scoffs. I have heard the sizzle of contempt in his spittled speech. I don't flinch from it.

Instead, I will tell you what she was like. Of course, I have to tell you what she feels like here and now, or I would only be remembering, and no longer the credible witness that I certainly am. Therefore I speak scrupulously in the present tense. That is to say, I must speak of the arousal of my organs in which the shimmer of her presence can be felt here and now, though it may make you uncomfortable to hear it and to know that you yourself are the spark of my flaming narration.

You are standing over me. You stand close enough to me now that the breath of your question is a quaver of intimacy like that which rustled in her fingers when she touched me through the steely inseam of my trousers. Think of it. *You* bring her into play with the parts of me that knew her best. In a manner of speaking, she is here with us.

So let me perform the introductions in excitements of sensation that rely less on memory than on physical reflex. Here and now it is a flexure that needs no muscle other than the words with which I have to tell you: she was like the rope that burns in my groin, to be pulled so sharply through the grip of my self-possession. *Now.*

It occurs to me her legs must have been shorter than yours, because when she stood before me, when she stepped towards me, her breath hovered in a hollow of my chest, while the misty jet of your speech—I feel it across my scalp, the reminder that her breathing came lower down on my anatomy—is nonetheless identical to the sensation that bristled under my baldpate as her respiration went faster against my heart. Do you sense it?

Of course I am sitting down and you are standing. And we are only talking. But we will both deduce that I am recollecting our—hers and mine—preferred position for the act of love: her legs straddling my thighs. What other recollection fits the facts of these sensations as I relate them to you here and now? What other pose fits the facts? Can you deny that my blind man's touch reaches as far back in time as you might wish to lead me on the tactility of these pulsing buds of sensation?

So you see, I have a kind of memory, which relies on being present in the present. And can the present fail to be a more reliable source of knowledge than conventional memory, especially for those who worry the grassiness of flesh and blood, for those who think too readily of murder?

Though the blood might rush to your head from possession of such a body as she held out to me then, your thoughts, like mine now, would soak into the mauve plush of her groin. A curiosity of the pleasure that draws the length of me into the teeth of my trouser zipper right now, as we speak of her groin, is the nibbling sensation which, suddenly, I know again is produced by a double set of labia: a proud secret of her sexuality. It was an aberration of her anatomy that you can confirm from the medical records you have no doubt already solicited. And then you'll want to know: is the memory you must attribute to my statement of this most obscure anatomical fact a source of the arousal I testify to here and now, or is arousal itself the sole cause of such a memorable sensation?

I nuzzle the same question in my thoughts of her. But you wouldn't deny all empiria? The sensations are unequivocal. And with them I seem to touch her body. I feel it as the physical weight that pushes even harder against the cloth of my inseam. Memory's leash strains against your credulity too, does it not?

Then kneel. Put your lips closer to my heart and perhaps I can tell you more of what you want me to remember. Let the flickering of your questions throw the shadows of her body even more tumultuously on my mind.

But what? You won't give me your knee? It doesn't matter. I am bumped by another sensation because, refusing to kneel, you have turned your flank against my shoulder and so turned her buttocks into the gravitational field of my own kneeling memory. My fingertips begin to pulse with a grip that must have fallen on her rotating hips. Or why do my hands motion involuntarily toward a squeeze? The blush of a warm cheek melts in my curled palm.

So now you also know that we were not the creatures of a single posture in what you might call our unimaginable lovemaking.

Now you feel my hand on your knee. Though you are standing and though you are half turned away, even from my desire to answer the question that you have just pressed upon me with such vehemence, you cannot escape the more vivacious impress of sensation that is my unrelenting grip. My volition is your involuntary memory.

Then know that the feeling of your bony knee evokes for me nothing less than the prodding snout of her sex, licking the salt from my hand. I feel her pubic bone where you refuse to bend. Can you deny that, though the knee is yours, I feel it too? And all of this should tell you, with the certainty that it is your professional duty to witness, that I have loved her, as I say.

Or do you say we weren't intimate? Then how else do you explain the violence with which you have broken my hold on this thought? Your knee. My thought. What would convince you that her pubis—groin bone slick inside the jowl cheek of that tenderest skin—was the head of a dog to my warm pat, and—here and now—favors the feel of your knee as if it were *your* familiar? Haven't you examined the body on the cold morgue slab? Couldn't you note there what I note here in the palm of my hand? I will bet the investigative tips of your fingers are themselves already printed on the series of black and white photographs meant to be a map of the deed that you wish me to confess is also my crime. If each part of the body is part of a puzzle to the investigating eye, pick this one out and hold it against the pattern of my recollection, as I tell it to you here and now. See if the head of the dog looks back at you, a sidelong glance from the shadowy inside of her thigh. Would you shrink from public corroboration of my most private knowledge?

And if you have already seen the place on her body where your lens left the lap of its wet tongue in her lap, you might feel the truth of what I tell you here and now, and feel it even as a weakening in the knee. Her body was a place for me. Believe it.

Here and now I have shared this place with you, intimate as the details of your own anatomy. And, good as my promise, it makes a perfect fit with your own recollection of the facts of the case as I have just reminded you of them. Didn't I tell you? Even a man without memory can remember, if the things of the present present a vivid enough form for fondling the past.

Because you have the shapes of her body, exactly as I described it, in your own flickering eye, because the coroner's bleak photographs of that body—pierced with red arrows and shackled with red circles to help you find your place—are your own memory of what I am telling you here and now, you must know that I have seen what you have seen. The phosphorous glare of the coroner's flash bulb illuminates nothing less than the verity of my own mind. Does it not?

And if I have seen her naked self so candidly can I have been anything but her lover—or her doctor?

Surely I would be her doctor if you were to credit the vile aspersions cast by our irritable young man upon the suitability of my old body for loving the more vibrant flesh of a younger woman. If you feel yourself ministering to that thought have every assurance that I would happily enroll you as my second patient.

Our festering fossil describes his own lust for her body, not the body itself. Her body, I can tell you, does not depend on any similarity with *his* sensations. I don't have to fall on the knees of anyone else's experience to prove my intimacy with her. My memory doesn't have to prop itself on the crutch of some muscle rousing excitement improvised out of the sensations of the present moment. I am capable of testimony that is the artifact of a proper past. I don't impersonate her flesh. I can exhume it.

And then you will remember that she is dead, which might recall you more purposefully to the duties of the investigation that are yours by law—and him to the punishment that awaits him, should you prove faithful to those duties. Are you faithful?

The proof of what I will tell you here and now is that I can give you a picture that is not merely *like* the photographic evidence you slip out of its gray sateen envelope—as soundlessly as the steel drawer that rolls upon the velvet orbits of perfect ball bearings, from the vaulted wall of the morgue—but one that is as good as the light that lets the camera see what it shows.

And let me shed the light where she was fully clothed, so that you will know that I am not stumbling in the darkness of desperate supposition, like him, our fat faker. The reliable anatomist exhibits a photographic memory, wouldn't you agree?

The tooth-shaped scar between the navel and the pubis was not the mark of the dog whose head the professor conjured so absurdly to your willing hand. There is a story here that only she could tell. I can listen.

Can you?

The scar is barbed like a hook. She might have been the fish on a line where she was caught by her father's careless casting, the rod dipped too low into the body of the boat. She had turned to the sound of his cursing the ripples on the water. She was six years old and wearing only a bathing suit. So the skin underneath was already puckered for the kiss of glinting metal. She told me there was a burst of pain, as if a balloon had snagged a nail.

But I know such stories are beyond your powers of corroboration. So I will stick to the physical parts of the case.

The storied scar is the only flaw on the skin that is gathered between her legs along tightly rolled seams. Its smoothness there, because it is hairless as well, plumps like a pillow. If I lay my head there in her lap it makes a perfect fit in the cradle of her pelvis. Snug from chin to crown. Measure my head if you doubt my word.

Still too subjective you say?

Then at the periphery of the aureole that crowns her left breast, look for a single pale hair that once I mistook for the tickle of my own eyelash. This is eyewitness testimony, though with my face buried in the heave of her chest, you might imagine there was nothing for me to see.

You can see it that clearly? Can you not?

Do you know she has an extra rib? Count from the bottom on both sides and you will tabulate the asymmetry.

Then there is a brown mole as high on the inside of her left thigh as the thumb can go to still close a grip on her buttocks.

And if you were drawing her head towards the readiness of your own lips, your fingers would discover a surprisingly deep trough where the wave of her hair comes to its towering crest in the palm of your hand.

There is a solitary black freckle on thc under lid of the clitoral hood. There is a pinprick of whiteness that gleams against livid tissue like a sprouting tooth where the right labia may be pried away from the pith of the vagina. There is a breath of dark brown hairs that whispers the hint of a vestigial tail where the crevice of her buttocks beckons. Who else but the lover knows these particulars of the case?

With the tweezer scrutiny of your blinking eyes, collect each of these items for your evidence bag.

But wait. The physical fact that will confirm my deepest intimacy with her body will be found adhering to the uterine wall. It is no bigger than a fingernail clipping you might have taken as your prize piece of evidence. Scraping along the edge of the fingernail, your forensic experts would expect to dig out the flesh of her assailant on the supposition that there would have been a struggle to the still unexplained death. A clue to faceless identity.

Under the fluorescent meniscus of your white-coated assistant's microscope, what adheres to the uterine wall will appear to have the eyes of a frog. Understand that I am the prince whose fetal self bulges within the eye of the frog, but whose identity cannot be spied beneath the most powerful lens you are capable of turning upon it in your laboratory.

You must kiss the frog to find out.

× × × × ×

You want to hear the ballyhoo of my first find on Blackman's Heath? You wish it from my own lips? The banner discoveries? You wish to see the photographs for the record? Touch the ribbons and the medals? You wish to hear the nostalgic song of my professional fame? I would not deny your glorying in the vicarious adventures of my gloried past.

But ask yourself, how could *I* summon it? And how could you trust my memory to resuscitate the body of the young archeologist that groaned and sighed, birthing the coldest human remains from the narrow ditches of this heath more than thirty years ago, if you will not credit my embrace of that infinitely more limber body which I still insist did warm to my sensitive touch not three days ago? Need I repeat, I may be a man without memory, but I am not a man without love.

I do know my fame. But it is like a rare coin at the bottom of a rarely opened draw. It is there for me to handle. I tickle myself with the glint of it turning in the palm of my shaky hand. But that forgetful hand has to fish for it. What bait would you be using then?

No, let this young man tell it. Roscoe Taste is my enemy. But Kraft Dundeed is his prototype. He wouldn't deny it. So we are co-conspirators in the story we would tell, like it or not. After all, who knows better the mastery of the master than the one who has chafed under the tutorial yoke? Who would know better the reasons one begs to carry my shovel, to cool my canteen, what pleasures can be wrung from the sweat-rag with which he was only too willing to soak up my thought-furrowed brow? Who would know better the reasons for such slavish behavior than the embittered slave? And of course Mr. Roscoe Taste could say more astutely than any man he bested to be my best assistant what methods distinguished me from those other fruitless laborers in the excavated fields. Didn't he tell you? He could have chosen from a vast array of other tutors to the trade. Surely my methods are what make me a man to model with. He knows my methods. He has studied me from afar and from as close as you yourself like to stand in the belief, no doubt, that physical proximity elicits a more truthful answer to your most probing questions.

Do give him a chance to speak for myself. It is no more than that which he already presumes to be naturally entitled to, as a man possessed of an unforgettable memory. Faultless. It could be no fault of his own, that he remembers so well what I must have forgotten, to tell it so differently from him.

Ask him how the story begins that it ends so badly. Ask him if the gold dust that brightened his fingertips when he picked the name of Kraft Dundeed to apprentice under, will leave an imprint as radiant as my own in the annals of our memory profession. Or will they merely match those fingertips imprinted in blood on our victim's throat, the most ornate incrimination of the guilty hand?

Pull your chair up to Roscoe's slim side. Hang on his lip. Give yourself the advantage of a sound faculty for nostalgic cogitations. He can tell you what you say you need to know of my professional life, because it is the host of his most parasitic longings. He is fastened to it with the orgasmic fervor of the lover whose embrace becomes a claw upon the oblivious flesh of his yielding partner.

The parasite that kills its host is not an unknown perversion of nature's plan. It is typical of the knowledge that does not come naturally.

x x x x x

FIELD INVENTORY: (April 21, 1954) Specimen # 1, Crate #1

Female of childbearing age. 1 meter, 22 centimeters. Wrists lashed in posterior position. Knees locked beneath chin. Ankles cinched together beneath buttocks. Hemp cord drawn up tightly through the cleft of the buttocks, along the spine to fasten first at the hands and then at the neck. No evidence of strangulation. Torsion of shoulder against pelvic axis marked in asymmetrical orientation of breasts. Toes flexed occipitally. Jaw awry. Mouth and trachea engorged with peated earth. Excavator notes: "the earth around the head is carved out, as if the victim had attempted to eat her way out of the grave."

Accompanying plaster cast of the cavity surrounding cranium exhibits striations consistent with human mandibular action and dental architecture.

× × × × ×

Of course everyone knows who Kraft Dundeed was, in his heyday. I say it deliberately to remind you that all of his glories are in the past where even he can no longer lay hands on the palpability of such a life. Buried in the past, well out of reach. Do you take my point?

And still it is a career to admire, especially as we have the distance of time to protect us from any vile touch.

Kraft Dundeed's greatness in the bogs was conferred at an early age. "Born to the grave," he liked to say, rattling his shovel saber-wise over his head, a swart general leading the charge upon the waiting field. His bald head always appeared molten in its brazen exposure to the sun. Even in this cold and fog-lapped dimness it shone with a temperature above the boiling point.

Need I persuade you that the flame has gone out in that head?

But, in those early days, his fatness was still unsprung within him. His physique was still clenched to the bone of a strapping frame. He was known for a prodigious digger, a ravenous walker, a man who could stoop for days in a bog and then stand up straighter than when he went down. An unerring nose for the truffles of our trade. But some cavilers caviled: "more an adventurer than a scholar." From the first imprint of his boot in the mire of discovery, he was just the man to figure such fame as followed those footsteps. And so many of us did.

His first institutionally supported dig was the landmark of a career that still arrays itself around him like a vast territory held under the intractable sway of a legal deed. Yes, officially he is the law of that land. Haven't I said he is the owner? The heath is his.

But *Dirtmouth* was the deed. His first find.

He confesses that he gave her that name. He protests that it was an homage to the manner of her death, which he insists was her own, despite what was meted out to her by her tormentors. A name tendered not out of mockery, but out of respect. The one hundred specimens collected in that twelve cubic meters of precisely quadranted peat-land were told to be the first such archeological findings in the history of famous digging. Foraging for a grain market, the first expeditionary team had come, quite surprisingly, upon a place of punishment.

So she was the first to shine under the light of Dundeed's shovel. She had been buried alive like all the rest, yet to be discovered. But she was the unique specimen. And the respect Dundeed said he owed her was beckoned, so he also told me, by the life force that so radiantly disfigured her face. As hamstrung as was the body in its hempen bonds, her face seemed to be in motion still, nine hundred years after the first clods were cast against her breath.

The open eyes were still bursting with the sunlight they would not release from their relentless gaze. The snarl of her lip bulged with a pebble lodged grievously against the gum. The pebble had unsheathed the front teeth—bitten and discolored as fingernails. I have studied her myself through the thick lenses of her glass case. Surely she would have clawed the sky if the hands had not been bound behind her back, dangling a helpless tickle above her coccyx. But the jaws were clenched to make up for the uselessness of the hands. The chin spiking forward made the whole head seem a furious tool in the grip of the most desperate labor.

And yet what spoke most vehemently of the frantic pitch of activity—it might have shattered that skull had it thundered upon her from the hand of another—was the truncheon rigidity of the throat. It was so tightly packed with earth matter that a visible extrusion rose like a thick, black grub upon the root of the tongue. The tongue itself stood straight out as if it had been trod on by the heaviness of the human foot that would have sealed her fate in any case.

"Dirtmouth." Curious how unimaginative Dundeed can be. But the museum-goers still catch their breath to see the physical frenzy that seems, even now, not to be completely stifled. They wonder what sin could be so unrepented. Seeing their own breath mist on the glass panes of the exhibition case they feel the pressure of the earth against their faces, and perhaps they know that neither will they ever breathe freely again.

If Kraft Dundeed had been the sculptor who chiseled this figure of strife from the most obstinate stone on the face of the earth, he could not have earned more notoriety for his artfulness.

Or I should say: "Artfulness indeed!" This is his reputation—though he would say it is just smoke from the fires of professional jealousy: that he is a theatrical producer more than an archeologist. *Dirtmouth* would have been the first recruit to his select repertory company, first to the footlights, his doyenne.

He played her on the stage of the most lurid popular imaginings. She appeared in the newspapers even before her dates and her coordinates on the excavator's grid appeared in the NATIONAL REGISTER OF ARCHEOLOGICAL FINDINGS. There was a cropped photograph, a veritable portrait. And she had things to say to the press. In Dundeed's ventriloquizing voice, of course. Spokesman for the Society. It came out as gnomic pontifications about indomitability and certain death. Indomitable rhetoric. A blather of inevitables. He gave her a family as well as a name. He gave her a motive for her crime. He would have no dissenting that there had been a crime to justify such a punishment. He declared her an adulteress. A child-mother. A woman capable of killing her own infant. "Not a drop of water in those eyes to soften the heart of a cudgeling judge," Dundeed whinged to the papers. Dundeed was the voice of her story, so that its meaning might be instantly clear to anyone with the credulity to peer through glass.

Then, in his account of what must have preceded her execution, smiling into the iridescent flash of the camera, Dundeed made her stand naked before a tribunal of three stooped men in hairy robes, shouldering unwieldy wooden mallets, wearing goat masks, touching horns when they nodded their agreement. Didn't I tell you he had the imagination for it?

He explained that their condemnation forced her to her knees, a posture more suitable for binding her in the prescribed manner. Kraft Dundeed pointed out that any struggle of the hands or feet would have burned against the offending organ, the coarse fiber of her bondage was so tightly drawn across the fascia of the pelvic saddle.

He held out a forbidden possibility: that for a woman like this, the dance of death would be only one more twitch of the lustful body for which this punishment was meted out. If the rope burned, it would have been only a spark of the fire that was already aflame where the kiss of the rope was hottest.

No doubt Kraft Dundeed could have acted the archeologist if he had wished. He could have demurred the showmanship, the confetti-lighted spectacle. He could have gone into the ground hushed with the sobriety of science. Instead he chose, as he put it, "to raise archeology from its silent gravesite." His genius—and I have never meant for you to doubt it for an instant—his genius was to think that archeology itself was as much in need of the excavator's spade as the buried bone. The proof is, we chew it still.

And within months of his discovery it was as if the money came out of the ground from a strike at gold instead of carbonized vegetable matter, and the flesh of that flesh which has in common with it only the dingy tint of dirt.

"Natural mummification is a mimicry of the earth," Dundeed loved to say. It was his belief that memory, like acting, was the most desperate form of mimicry. He claimed that his financial backers were paying to remember all that time had forgotten. In that way they might become more like the earth, without going into it themselves. He said they wished to immortalize themselves by burrowing back into the womb of time. But, such fancied thoughts were not harbored by the swaggering archeologist himself.

Dundeed himself thought of the oily brown limbs of the find site, made malleable by the compression of the earth, as nothing more than the soft turds of time. He said it was time straining to ease itself of the impossible burden of the past, delivering them, with barely a grunt from the man with the shovel, into the wide-eyed present.

But you wouldn't expect a man without memory to credit the past for what it was instead of what it *is*. "He brings them so vividly to life" was the abiding accolade of his career.

Kraft Dundeed's most celebrated finds have always been ticklish to the touch of his discovering hands. They come alive to the moment of their discovery. And no one can deny it. They are marvelously resuscitated in the breathless announcements Dundeed himself purveys to the daily newspapers, always a photographer ready to hand. The specimens are anointed with names that beg to tell their stories: *Oat Grubber* buried with a strangled duck; *Snailhead*, with phosphorescent eyes swimming in the undulant pitch of a bronze helmet; *The Jealous Brothers* buried together, the one with all of his limbs hacked from the trunk, the other with the extra limbs lashed to his torso like weights thrust upon a drowning man.

All, as I said, ticklish to his touch. Barely *unearthed*—and remember we tender the term gingerly with bog people—they were already convulsed with Kraft Dundeed's imaginings of those details of an ancient life—the grislier the better—which might excite the mind that swims in the current of forgotten times. Bard of the bog, he plucks their limbs for a note to carry the sound of his own voice. And so he makes them accompany his song. Each one a garishly limber marionette flailing away in the widening repertoire of the *maestro's* bog playlets. More popular with every performance. Entertainment for all who have a head for darkness, dampness, digging: "The three d's of archeology," as Dundeed calls them.

These little d's are, as you will have already guessed, only the stuttering intimation of the capital "D" that tolls so blackly in the thoughts of Kraft Dundeed's most effusive benefactors, the patrons of his unearthing equipment: his trucks, his tractor, his back hoe, his sifters and scanners, his x-ray projector. All the expensive prosthetic devices of the trade which come to life when the spirits of finance are roused by a titillating tale that could only be told by the dead. Just ask Mr. Levant Doyle and his black-and-white-striped-vested associates. Dundeed's financial backers are the lively shadows thrown by the grandiose gestures of his success. They are the hidden benefactors of the light that shines upon Dundeed's career.

And we do not forget Dundeed's marbled museum. Endowed by Mr. Doyle and his associates. It is built of large green stones that would serve as well for the real mausoleum which it is only the historically accurate allusion to. Names are incised over classical architrave to honor the donors of each room. As you might expect, each room is more a theatrical setting than a reputable exhibition space. The figures floating in their glass cases are animated in the poses of their ultimate asphyxiation. If we are struck by the illusion of movement it is certainly because we are sucking up the air in which they are so starkly revealed to us, gasping. They are made scintillatingly visible to us in that empty space which our minds must fill with blackest dirt, if we were to remember how they died.

Which is to say, I admit it, we who attend are all players by the rules of Dundeed's game. We have our parts, if we are not full partners in the performance.

I don't deny or disown my resentments.

But I frankly accuse him. I accuse him in the name of Archeology.

Not only because for him the past is too much present and so that much more bereft of the past, but because such thoughts as he purveys are only too congenial to the mind of a killer. They must be tracked.

I'm sure you take my meaning.

The past made too vividly present is the death of the dead past, isn't it? Life-likeness isn't a fault of the mummy herself. My point is: can a man who thinks so lightly of bringing the dead to life worry that slackening of the puppet string which lets the outstretched limb fall back to earth?

Of course everyone knows who Kraft Dundeed was. Now let's remember who he *is*.

× × × × ×

You say I had a wife? You wonder if there was a child in the bargain?

Then that would be two of them missing. From the untidy domicile of my recollection I mean. I don't remember.

But I have my book.

You wouldn't have guessed it yourself. So now you have another clue by which to deduce my unstinting honesty.

It is my *Memory Book*. My book remembers what I have forgotten. My book remembers me to myself.

Which is why, when I call upon my *Memory Book*, you should appreciate that I humble myself as if to the leather straps and aluminum struts of a physical prosthesis. The cripple is so resentful of his crutch.

But I have not yet given you proof of my humility. And for this reason I am happy to part the covers of my book for you. Beyond that, it may tell you what you wish to know.

It will tell you that my humility began with the first faltering steps of my memory. In fact, they are the first recollections to tread upon the pages of my book. Since the first thing it knew was what it thought I would forget, my book begins in the real past. Everything I could remember then is present here as a memorial to the moment when I first comprehended that forgetfulness would be my future. Forgetfulness was already lapping at my shore.

And yet, my book, itself as heavy as the last brick that would seal up the wall between the present and the past, is only the cenotaph, memorializing the advent of my forgetfulness. Because, slipped from the clutching bonds of that older self who wrote it, I am now another man, however much older and even more decrepit to appearances.

For I am younger too, as I have already told you. Measuring by the brevity of the memorable past that precedes me, I am a veritable child and certainly a minor to the letter of that law by which you would sentence me to absolute posterity.

Which is to say that though I myself am not entombed within these pages, still it is a kind of tomb. Each day recorded in memorialization of what will be forgotten raises the present as a greater and greater edifice over the past. The present heaping upon itself stones freshly hewed from time's inexhaustible quarry, in that way belies the purpose that lies within its makeup. Out of the past it makes up the greater part of the present. That is how my book is made. One crisp page after another.

Flutter the pages on the bevel of your perusing thumb and they present a surface as smooth as the unscalable face of a pyramid in the distance. Nevertheless each page is an entry and so an entrance. Here is one. But remember, you enter a tomb that has long since been pilfered of its real treasure:

Did I plan to marry Sophia Pasthand for her clever relation to time? She was much older than myself, at twenty-six. I was twenty-three. Having come precociously into her family legacy—a father's early death makes time seem breathless—she was poised to underwrite the depths of my first digging. She could afford to make me the man I was meant to be well before my apprenticeship at the university had formed the image of him. She offered a wedding gift. Payment in full for a year's spade work.

Yes. A wedding in an excavated barrow was all that she solicited in return. I gave it gladly. Wasn't I in love? Doubly: the damsel and the dirt! We made up a hasty wedding party out of our cadre of "gravediggers." So did we jovially refer to ourselves, those of us who stayed loyal to the find site on weekends and holidays. All of us passionate students at the university. All of us haloed with brilliance. But only some destined for the great discovery. We nevertheless made up a society. Could there be better testimonial to the solidarity of society than a wedding?

I remember the gold awning vaulted above our heads when Sophia and I were ready to step down into the ceremonial chamber. A moment before we had squinted under a real dome of golden sunlight. The day had dawned unusually gleaming for such a dimly lit land. A match for one another's slenderness, our shadows—Sophia's and mine—had momentarily stood apart from one another as the hands of a clock about to tell another time.

One seldom sees one's shadow in the bog lands. You would think—on that basis alone—there should be no confusion between what is real and what is only imagined for the moss-footed among us.

Now Sophia and I advanced into the sodden gloom to take our vows. Our friends hailed us from below with an allergic grating in their voices. Their fists were clenched with rice. Sophia and I looked at each other with metallic eyes in that sun-glaring moment before the shade came down.

We descended from the brace of jittery wooden steps onto spongy ground. For a moment we needed sea legs to stand. We wobbled between the two rows of our expectant friends. I didn't recognize a single face. My knees watered with the bobbing of the improvised floorboards that made a gangplank in the direction of the priest.

That's when the whispering began in my ear. She was making a plea. She had something in mind. Sophia implored me to imagine that the unnatural buoyancy of the earth—this after all had been her plan—was the heave of a mother's labored breathing. So confident she was of a propitious birth. How like Sophia to convert the reality of a tomb into the illusion of a womb for this event. And we, the married couple, were meant to be its issue. The surround of richly humidified turf, the soft ooze of darkness around the spearheads of candlelight did in fact evoke some flickering knowledge of the womb which we would nevertheless never mistake for the feat of remembering.

Notwithstanding, that is of course what I am about at this very moment. I'm about to write that I remember Sophia's grasp of my flinty hand. She held it fast to her flank. Pulling it slowly along the contour of her thigh, she gathered enough friction from the silken weave of the wedding gown to remind me that the current of smoothness running beneath it was the free flow of her whitest skin. Remembering that the wooden braces arched over our bowed and murmuring heads were like nothing so much as the ribs of a capsized hull, I thought again how much Sophia wished me to think of water and fetal bobbing, in order to be born the perfect husband.

Certainly for the two flanking rows of our guests who must have worried the feeling of their feet becoming immobilized in the muck of their muddy boot prints and for the priest, compulsively licking the bristles of his moustache, blotting the moisture that beaded up continuously in an atmosphere that fogged his lips, the hastily converted barrow was as inhospitable to the notion of fresh womb-life as the fungal tang that tainted our every indrawn breath. However uncomfortably, we awaited the invocation of higher forces and the commencement of the happy ritual.

But at my side Sophia, unsteadily buoyant with the motion that swam in her head, suddenly let her knees buckle under her. She let the passionate undertow of her fancy snatch her from my grip. It happened in a wave action that left her prone upon the trestle boards where we stood to take our vows, now wobbling more than ever against the unsteadiness of the moisture in the ground. The words "I do" became a shrill spray on my lips, before anyone had formed them in their thoughts of what should happen next. Was it the breath of my words that blew her away?

The bride was prostrated at my feet. My hand swung empty at my side. The priest choked upon the crumbly syllables of his unformed words. The air blanketed us with a silence as dense as mold spore.

The commotion that then fell upon Sophia's spread-eagled form seemed as much a tidal effect of the wave that had felled her as a rescue. And at the bottom of that wave trough before the would-be rescuers' outstretched arms and hands could close upon wrists and ankles to raise her, rinse the foam of confusion from her body, Sophia began to move in a way that made the helping hands freeze in their fingertips.

Still leaning forward in the posture of their beneficent intent, each one of the circle of wedding guests took one step back. By this motion they appeared to be hauling the sunken weight of a sea net from shallow waters. At the center of their circle and just breaking the surface of my vision, as I peered over the rim of stooped shoulders, the prostrated bride appeared to be trying to give birth. I can remember how the thought pulsated against the backs of my eyes. I know I can remember because, here and now, the quaver of déjà vu almost makes the page upon which I am writing these words crumple under the pressure of the pen with which I am now transcribing the event—and with all the detail that is bustling at the exit doors of my capacity to remember what it was like.

And I know it is bona fide memory because my vision is not yet putrefying with the stickiness of "like." I do not explain it.

It was exactly what it was to see:

The lace hem of Sophia's gown foaming between her legs, her knees furiously knocking the air. She was shucking her naked pelvis from the voluptuous fit of the gown as if only—so I thought—to have something to deliver of such burdensome contortions.

So at last I was the only one to reach into the net, the only one to approach her, stooping, stepping as gingerly as if making my way across a rocky shallow. The others ebbed further into stricken poses of revilement. One threw out a hand to draw me back, but reeled it in before it hooked me, as if I were already lost to the slippery slime of whatever they recoiled from.

Indeed Sophia did pull me down. Or her bodily upheaval overwhelmed the precarious balance of my stooping. There had been something written so small in the snarled lines of her face that it had wanted a closer eye. That is why I didn't see the club action of the skull sprung from behind her face when I peered into its complications.

The blow was an exploding vision of what all the others had already seen. She struck me down to her level. The physical dislocation I experienced then was such that my head might have been kicked to her feet. My trunk lay where my own feet had stepped out from underneath it.

Then, able to move only my head, rocking it in the soft furrow of earth which had been kicked up in its path, my thoughts lying so far from my sprawling limbs, I felt oddly in scale with the dense tarry loaf which my one eye, free of the dirt, could now see Sophia was forcing between her shuddering legs. Unswaddled as a sheaf of tobacco leaves, it was immediately recognizable as the mummy of an eight- or nine-month-old bog bairn, unearthed from a leather sack less than a week before.

Now I was staring at its contents, my mouth as slack as the opening of the sack itself. I was helpless. I knew I was helpless. I merely waited for my own head to roll at the approaching footstep. Waited for the first touch of the toes. Waited for the moment of surprise, the pause of inspection, waited to experience the crunching silence of being something underfoot. I waited for the sound of the hand fisting itself in my hair, the swing of the arm, the arc of motion that would fling me against the solid wall of the barrow, expectant of what might be shattered from within.

The smile that shrieked across her mouth then might have slit my throat for the way it took my breath away. I remember nothing else. Only awakening in a feverish cot, a day too late to know what had really happened. She was already gone.

How artful that the first last memory of my book should be of a woman fashioning a memory for me. Certainly it is no artifice of my own. In this case, I am only the one who is remembering. By decamping promptly on the heels of the event—in the primal morning hours when those who watched her bed had themselves slipped into a tumult of dreams—Sophia Pasthand consigned me to my memory. She consigned me to memory, as one commits a patient to the venerable asylum for those who will only know what they can never understand.

No. Sophia Pasthand never became my wife, though the conception of a living child is a thing for me to ponder. The reports were that she had delivered—a live, pink child—on the continent. The conception of the child was dated (by those of our intimate friends with the wit to calculate it) roughly to the day of her disappearance: the day after the ceremony that was not consummated. But, of course, we two had ravenously consummated our desire on the day before the wedding ceremony was so unpropitiously undertaken. So there is no problem with that deduction.

And yet it remains a deduction from an airy premise. For it is only her absence that I can be sure of. Surely it is her absence that serves my memory. I recall my lonely inventory of our vacant love nest: the turquoise sandal with a torn ankle strap, lost in the middle of the bare floor, the empty dresser drawers lolling at the furthest extension from their gaping frames, a minute cairn of nail clippings (fingers or toes?) marking the distance from the unused waste basket, waiting a dozen footsteps across the unprinted floor from it. She left it all behind.

These things that are fasten the memory of what is not. This thing Sophia did was meant to imprint her absence. She knew what she was doing. The stone that is flesh for the fossil vertebrae does suffice to breathe life into our thoughts of its existence. We seize hold of what holds our attention.

Now it is the pen between my fingers.

I will tell you what Cinna was like because she was like someone else whose caress was my cradle. I must be loveable to be so loved, don't you think? And generous to permit your investigative hands delving into the depths of the cradle for a tickle of what you are searching out.

I said she was a young woman. My mother too had her youth when she had me. I'm sure I remember the smoothness of the skin around her mouth and the sheen of her green eyes when she held me up to her face to coo at me. The lustrous profusion of red hair. Memory is such a mirror.

Nor, I can swear, did my mother wish me to grow older when she rocked me, letting her red tresses fall over my eyes, tickling a rib with her little finger. Singing breathily into my shining ear. Her voice tinkled like a silver bell around my neck. I was her little lamb. I like to think I still wear the pinkness of my infant self as a highlight of my mature flesh tone.

I preserve all the rest of it in my thoughts of her thinking of me, thinking of the featherweight of my cooing existence as something quite precious to hold. She never dropped me.

But she did fall herself. Stepping off the porch step with me bundled in her arms, her eyes became caught in a skein of sun glare that might as well have tangled around her ankles. For she was lifted up by her feet. I'm sure I remember a brief wingedness, a bird-chirp from her lips, and a landing, broken only by the splinters of both her elbows upon the slate walkway below. She saved me, they never tired of reminding me through all the sun splashed afternoons of my lingering childhood. She was my savior, they implored me to remember.

But she was not dead. No. It was me who seemed to die, or so I'm told, and can only imagine, since I have no memory of the state of catatonia into which I had apparently been thrust. For six months my mother's plaster arms remained sculpted in the gesture of empty embrace, a fact which I am told I suffered as a great rebuke, and one not to be forgiven lightly. They say my eyes went empty as her arms. They would not hold her in their gaze. I sealed my lips in her presence, though I was too young to talk. And yet I taught myself the language of tears, making me both fluent with her grief and the uncommunicative up-stager of its arena. They say she was driven from my bawling presence, perhaps as if from the flooding compartment of a sinking vessel.

When she at last regained the use of her limbs, it was me she reached for first, however tentatively. They say I lay impassively in my crib, forcing her to test the extent of her recovery against a haul of dead weight. The weight of the world they said, if one were to judge by the stone face. And of course it was my head falling loose from her embrace that caused her—her reach already extended to its limit over the crib side—to juggle her grip. That was the more grievous injury for her. Not to let me drop a second time, doubled her pain.

The second splintering of her elbows wet my bedding. Or so they tell me. I remember tears falling on my lips. But my eyes were still closed to everything but the mewling sounds that remained trapped in her throat. Through my cracked lids I watched the soft skin of her throat heave against the silence.

They tell me she didn't drop me, though the ligaments tore away from the joint ends of the bones as they disintegrated, letting the frayed shafts fall with a taut bounce against the flesh that held them. Her elbows stabbed her from the inside.

The next nine months, in the care of surrogate mothers, aunts, neighbors, maids, saw me taking my first steps, opening outer distances for flight. They say I could never be found. I would be happened upon in a closet or clothesbasket (I was that small for my age), under a staircase or in the dank shade of the furthest tree from the house.

They say my mother's grief was profound. She lay at the bottom, as if she had tripped into its depths, though it was only the mattress of her marriage bed upon which she was sprawled, on her back, with the white plaster arms stiffly crooked above her head, as if she were still plummeting.

Though I was small enough to be carried when the saw and the hammer were finally applied to my mother's casts, I did not permit myself to be brought to her bedside. I remember waiting for her behind a dripping shrubbery, my tiny pink hands pressed into the front pockets of my pants. I remember the aromatic stiffness of the dressing in my combed hair, the twitching of my shoulder blades, the soft hum of my stomach inside my shirt, the feeling of my toes in my shoes. Everything waiting.

Everything waiting to be gathered up into her miraculous, long arms, whiter than the healing plaster and shimmering with the warmth in which I had first begun the contemplation of a happy state. This must be how I think of it now, though my memory of that presence of mind is as present as a catch in the throat.

They say she did descend the fateful porch step in a flutter of satin slippers, did discover me behind my shivering bush, did kneel down to sweep me into the reach of her nearly straightened arms.

But if this is true I have no memory of it. If it happened it is no more to me than a find in the peat, a piece of the past under the fingernails. Almost unthinkable.

I simply remember a resumption of my happy state like the recovery of a lost pulse to the physician's patient fingertip. I have ever been warm in my mother's embrace since. I am unembarrassed to say that I remain a warm egg of the nest however far flown from my home. Ticking away with no aspirations of hatching out, I am proud to be a mother's child with none of the pretensions of maturity. My mother always respected my immaturity. She has given the child his due, even when she has encountered him under the heaviest disguises of bearded cheek and hairy nostril, sweat and smegma. She always knew how to stoop to the level of the sandbox, to take a hand quietly in hand, and to elicit the voice of inexperience.

Cinna was like that, since you ask. It must be what drew her to me. An appreciation of what the child is capable of saying in the oracular voice of its innocence. She said I had a gift for tingling her spine with my words. It was the utter untrammeledness of my words she said. She seemed to breathe in expectation of what I might say.

I paused before I told her that she was my *find*, though I would never take a shovel to her. I would cherish her body, which my words would never touch. If she would heat the atoms of my body to the intensity of evaporation she would be free to treat me like a puff of smoke when she tired of the effort. She smiled at the winsomeness of such imagination.

They say my mother smiled before her fall. And because it was a thing that could not be mended, she kept the pieces of that smile in her apron pocket along with the scrap of rag she used to wipe the lipstick from my cheek.

Who are *they*, you ask? Aunts, uncles, family confidants. Bosoms of the family. Those who love me not as well as my mother, but enough to make my mother wonder if I could love them more.

No, not Cinna. Mother.

When you ask how I met her you are asking how a nose sniffs to its scent. I met her in the dirt, where everything else of value to me has seemed to lie in wait. Or was it just waiting? Everyone says I sniff to the dirt like the proverbial pig to his grimy truffle. But it might be truer to say that the dirt finds me in my exploratory crouch. She did.

She brought me a skull. She called down to me in my crouch. I was trawling the bottom of a trench in which we had just that morning sieved specimens of human teeth, scattered like chicken feed. When I lifted my head—above ground level and to the level of her boot—she presented her gift even before she presented herself.

She knew I would recognize the skull to be as much a password of professional introduction as the Bronze Age man himself, who would have kept a short chin and the eyes of a ferret under the twitch of his furry brow. She stooped to shake my hand. Only then did I see that this young man, who is so sullenly hunched between us now, was standing behind her then—apparently the door through which she had passed to my acquaintance. He was standing too stiffly upright, blotting the light over her shoulder.

Did she fall or was she pushed? One might even ask, did she jump? How then was she suddenly in my arms before I could even get off my knees? For a heartbeat she hung around my neck. Then the bough broke and we fell together in what could easily have been taken (I do not say mistaken) for a carnal embrace.

There in the bottom of the trench I wondered if when I stood up again I shouldn't be picking up where I had left off with Sophia Pasthand. Cinna was as long, as lithe, and as resplendently tressed.

But I am getting too far behind myself you say. How do I remember to remember a past beyond my primary recollection, let alone what I am dredging from the trench? In this case, and once more, you are yourself my gallant *aide memoire*, remarking as you did, the curiosity that romance can blossom twice amid the shriveling specimens. It was no doubt the snide juices of your laughter in saying so that plumped your mouth into a resemblance to Cinna's full lips, which in their turn did kiss my recognition how Sophia's mouth puckered as perfectly. Once the surfaces of things begin to scintillate so mirroringly I can sometimes make the past recollect itself as an artifact of the unsullied present.

And wasn't Cinna smiling in my arms when we stood together in the trench? To be in my arms could even have been a rescue don't you have to think? Couldn't her smile have registered the gratitude for my readiness at the moment of emergency? Couldn't it be that she recognized me as the strong and able man against whom youth must still measure its muster? In any case, if she wished an introduction to the pater of her profession, wouldn't it have been out of the same good faith we place in all fathers, that they will never disappoint our expectation of strong arms? Fathers are lovers on the strength of the same arms.

In any case, this use of my arms would have required releasing my grip on the skull. To mention it, this thought is the clink of my recollection that the skull struck something as brittle as itself in the bottom of the trench. Wouldn't that sound have been reason enough for all of us to fall to our knees to commence sifting our eyes through the screen of bog crumbs that now included skull fragments: one eye socket broken out from the brow like a discarded monocle, splinters of septum, the rim of a cheekbone shivering with sharpness.

How perfect that the shards of one skull should ring out the discovery of another that might be excavated intact. The skull had shattered against the brow of another skull. Another find! Loss and gain! The harder head, nine-tenths buried and still impacted with spongy bog matter, would have absorbed the impact like a belated pulse of neandertal thought. When, after meticulous hours of digging, etching, brushing, blowing, Cinna held the second skull whole in her hands—darkness emanating from the eye sockets and the grin of the upper jaw gnashing the rag in which she was preparing to wrap this find—we all let ourselves come to rest around her kneeling form.

If I make the picture, you can see it. But it is yourself who reminds me so much of the skull. I make no discovery in saying that your brow is heavier than most. The black hair falls on your eyes. Your eyes, themselves, are dark enough to suggest their absence. I can imagine the bore of darkness receding into the furthest echo of consciousness in your head. And the wide nose, the full, almost dribbling lips, the roving whorl of facial hair, all help me to see Cinna sitting—ancient head in hand—in our circled midst with her great velvet brown eyes resting plush on myself.

I can see that she was looking at me as plainly as I can feel this tuft of lint on my lapel. As I have already said—do you recall it?—memory makes sense of sense in just this way. So the tickle of her eyes on my shivering cheek supplies another piece of evidence that you can puzzle out if you believe in our love at first sight. You would have seen it first.

And if you can see this as clearly as I relate it, wouldn't you know she must have planned her seduction from that moment?

You would read it in the dark contraction of her nostrils, the feathery motion of her tongue behind her teeth, not to mention the trembling skin at the base of her throat which must appear to be the hypnotic rotation of a tiny hip under a taut sheet. The faintest undulation of the flesh portends the weight of the whole body rolling on a wave of passion.

And if *you* can see it, couldn't we trust that the same recognition fell like the leaden folds of a funeral shroud over this fellow's beaming countenance?

Roscoe Taste had the sun in his face. I had her.

Judging from how pale he is now, you can imagine how painful such enlightenment might have been.

And so we might look for the first signs of motive grimacing in the knife-blade corners of his mouth as he realizes that he has just introduced her to the man who will pry her loose from his own covetous embrace: a fat man of years at that, bald, ungainly, a haze of yeast smelly about him. I can hardly believe it myself.

I'm sure nothing happened then, though the butter was already melting in the slow action of her hips, when she raised herself from the trench. She was mounted on her purpose and there was nothing more to be done.

Again, I don't say this from memory. But is it not a fair deduction from what we have already agreed to see together? We have seen it, have we not? Memory itself would be redundant.

And yet I do forget something. I forget to say that a bronze age head is not the easiest trophy to procure. The woman herself must have been descended from a family collection. And you must remember that collection is the greater part of recollection. Think of the picture of your rose-hued wife, so warmly pressed inside the fold of your wallet. I'm sure it's there, cropped to flatter her face. Is it not also a head? Doesn't that make you a collector as well?

× × × × ×

FIELD INVENTORY: (June 6, 1960) Specimen #1, Crate #14

Male head. 15 centimeters by 12 centimeters. Age twenty-one. Leather skullcap bunched at crown, laced under chin. One eye open. Dilated .32mm. Lips sewn shut. A faint shudder of skin abraded over the cheekbone. The head is tied in profile to a coarse muslin pillow, stuffed with heather. Three loops of heavy twine around the head are hitched in series under the cleat of the nose. The burl of the knot has gnawed at the already slightly depressed forehead. Mineral effacement has joined the resting cheek to the muslin sheath. The insertion of a paper-thin blade into that seam released a spray of dust. Identified preliminarily (by field chemist) as rose petal.

× × × × ×

Dundeed talks of what she saw in him.

Didn't I warn you of the puppet master's sly string? He makes Cinna move before your eyes as if she were alive. It is the trademark of a career: the liveliest movements of the corpse are meant to draw your eye to the even more limber exertions of the maestro who lurks behind. Never one to hide his artifice, Dundeed has ever counted on his audience's gravitation from the light. The brightest footlights, for him, shine backstage.

Let me tell you that Cinna was limber in her own right. And not one to use her eyes when a more grappling part of her anatomy would serve.

We met officially that way, grappling with a boulder that bulked in the path of our guide-wires. Marking off quadrants in a field. The excavator's blueprint. We had been jointly assigned the task of engraving the site with the coordinates of the search.

We drove our knees into the earth on either side of the gray obstruction. Because I felt the stone move first in the clenching of my groin muscles, I imagined she was in the grip of the same involuntary urge. I could see only the silent tapping of her kneecaps where daylight parted the rock from the earth beneath my hand. I heard her grunt.

When the boulder touched ground again it rolled enough to clear the space between us. But the grunt still rumbled in the air, as if it had been the lurid speech of the smile with which she greeted me from the far side of the stone.

I never guessed she would own it was her specialty: the grunting muscles of the groin. Cinna claimed command of all the grainy strands which could be focused in their lateral weave to stiffen the vaginal walls like a truncheon. She promised me that she moved inside herself, like a mysterious passage beyond the glassy stillness of her torso, where the eyes of her lover were bound to be left floating on the surface of credulity.

She could *hold her man*, so she would say. I do confirm it.

And when she chose to move the outside of her body she was as masterfully in control of the muscles that hinged to bone. She could bend from the hips without bending her knees, or lean as far backwards, so that the broad angular bones of her pelvis glistened under the thinness of the skin like wild facial gesticulations under water.

She could rotate her hips in so complete a half-circle that she was practically standing back to back with herself. It turns a man around to find his pleasure like that. And she could split herself in two with a deft pointing of her toes. She could lay those tips on opposite horizons like the spell casting nibs of magic wands. But of course the magic dazzled between her legs. There, I often felt myself to be the whirring shaft off an ever toppling gyroscope.

I am trying to convey the life of the body because her true lover would have to be a match for what that body could demand. I was a match. She was my flame, if I can be so witty to say so. And Dundeed's mind—with what all he conjures from it—is smoke to all that. Blow on this old fellow's mind and you'll see how it scatters. Cinna and I did not think about what we were doing in one another's arms, because we could do it. We did it.

I mean to say that our first coupling was memorable because it happened, not because I say it did. And it happened in this ancient's mildewed crypt of an office, where I admit I doffed the duties of the good assistant with my clothes.

She did know who Kraft Dundeed was. She touched his books before she touched my cheek. She let her eyes float in the murky glass displaying his professional certificates, as well as the photo-trophies of his most celebrated findings in the field. Image after image of him rising out of the mounded earth, slowly acquiring the appearance, if not the buoyancy, of a sea mammal, breaking the waves for breath. As his girth enveloped him in successive frames, his figure seemed to flatten, as if sinking into the photographic emulsion.

Why she wanted to sit in his chair, to pull the velvet collar of his smoking jacket off the coat rack and around her throat, to suck the end of his pipe, I couldn't tell you, except to say it was her chosen profession and he was the spitting image of it. To us all. I don't say I never peered into that dark glass myself.

But when she was through dusting the surfaces of his daily routine, oddly lost, for that brief time, in the motions of a bored housekeeper, I sensed she was ready to walk through the looking glass. From the other side, I stretched out my arms and she passed into the crush of my embrace.

Then the moment was sprung with three dimensions again, as I knew she preferred it to be. My body could make a proper space for the extravagant gymnastics of her ecstatic body. The perspiration stood out on my forehead in sympathy with the slick contortions by which she unknotted all the pinched sources of my pleasure. When, finally, we filled that space with the steamy breathlessness of our exhausted bodies, I felt sleep tumesce in me like the pressure of a hand that forces open a secret door. Did I dream?

I felt as if I had suddenly stepped into a room that had been sealed off from the outside world for donkey's years. It was as if nettles of dust and mold spore bristled in my sinuses to tell me of time passed in airless captivity. But I had just arrived, led, I surmised, by the hand of a stranger.

And yet I had needed to take no steps to enter this room. Nor could I see the door through which I would have to exit, if I was to know the way I had come.

Instead I realized I was my child self. And more. I was locked in the arms of another child. We were desperately entwined. Her tiny hand hewn in relief on my upper arm. Her sticky breath caught in the passageway of one ear like a clot of cooling sap. Our groins pressed to the hilt of one another's stabbing frenzy. Even our feet were wrapped one upon the other's raw instep as if a rough thumb had rolled over our separate strands, tangling us into a single thread.

Then I realized that I was not just dreaming. I was remembering. The bosomy heat of Cinna's close embrace was incubating a reverie of my most virginal sexuality.

They had called us children, we were so small. And though we were children by most standards of adult suspicion, we bridled with the strident indignation of bodies which, however miniaturized, were mature enough to speak past those words of sexual mystery through which the majority of children merely peer dimly into the distance of their adulthood.

Ours was a room inside a room, a closet space so tight that we could make it wet with our fervid speech. She seemed to cough her words in fits. Mine expanded like bubbles against the widening circles of her eyes. I blew upon her eyes to make them flicker. Our space held us that close. We named our desires before we performed their satisfaction. She called her body Cynthia. When she called me, Roscoe, it was as if I were a-wag with a tail I didn't know I had grown.

We were burrowed in our burrow when the frantic voices of parents could be heard like the pack in full pursuit. Our names rose from the surrounding wood like the speckle-winged prey the dogs were meant to carry in their soft, wet jaws.

Squirming against the rough-hewn confines of our hay closet, in the loft space of an abandoned stable, we might as well have been treed: we heard their heavy clambering up the ladder like the floor collapsing under our backs. When they fished long white arms into the black recess of our hiding place—where we became a tentacled frenzy of kicking and clawing—they blindly seized upon parts of both of us as one body. When one of them exerted his overwhelming strength we came apart in his squeamish grip and slithered separately free, recoiled into the warm concealment, kicking our nesting hay behind us.

They sucked on their curses. Spat after the winking disappearance of our knees and shins. They silently peered. A hush of whispering. And then the velvet billowing of a freshly ignited torch caught our ears. With that wind up we knew we would have to let ourselves be blown. Our naked bodies shot from the opening of the closet in a flurry of white parts, as if we imagined that by blurring their vision of us we could tip them off balance, pull them into a depth where they would surely lose their footing. Then we would leap to our escape.

Instead they stilled our commotion with the iron stiffness of their arms, a ratcheted tightening of the bones in their fists, as grim as the turning of the key in the lock. They made us stand in the whitening chill of what they called our shame while they doused us with the icy water of their rebuke. And then they emptied two wooden buckets over our heads.

When I was delivered, still naked and dripping with ice crystals, to my mother's open door—she stood with a blanket already unfurled in the blustering frame—they thrust me upon her as if they thought they could bare her own shame with the shock of my white limbs.

She merely swaddled me like the child I was. In her arms, I gave her good reason to kick the door closed behind us. Words, clearly meant to be hurled after her, sounded a click of broken teeth against the resonant planks after the door slammed behind us.

When she sat me in front of her she laid her eyes like green coins on my eyes. I heard the silence of her judgment like the grave in which her best thoughts of me were already buried. I awaited the deliquescent step of the grub and the snail for which the person in the grave is fit company. I held my breath in order to more appropriately inhabit the chamber of my faults.

To my amazement my mother then let the smoky warmth of her voice condense upon the chill of my contrition with a question that held in the air like a droplet about to burst.

"Can you show me where you touched her?"

Her hand seemed to be leading her voice to shape the question into a command when, just as unexpectedly, it moved to relieve me of the burden of obedience. For she proceeded to touch the places on her own body before my lips could form around the names. With each contact her eyes appeared to soften as if the green pupils were being palpated themselves by fingers of light.

Then she spoke of the places of the body and the visitations of love that pay them their due. She said it was right for me to undertake the journey, as I should think of it.

"But," she said, "the body of the young woman, for the young man (and the body of the young man for the young woman) is the map of the mother."

She said: "When the laughing needles of physical excitement prick the skin into such a state of liveliness that the whole body cannot resist being what it is, what else would one expect to find but the source of one's own love-making? The source of that lovely body? Mother's love makes love.

"To follow the map is to fondle the knowledge that once was found in the mother's heart when it was touched into life. After all, the mother's body moves too and in directions that defy the imagination of the one who lacks a map.

"The back can arch strenuously enough to seem to turn the navel inside out. The bottoms of the feet can turn away from the earth until the shoulders stand upon it. The knee can touch the chin the better to communicate with the quiver of a cleft buttock. The hips can swivel off the axis of the spine shedding gravity with the bone. The head itself can turn so far around it furrows the shoulder blades into wings that fly out of the corner of your eye.

"Each contortion clears a bigger space on the map to accommodate the arrival of the child into the womb of adulthood."

My mother's soft words molded themselves to the coiled shape of my hearing, in the way a person can be deafened by filling the ears with molten wax. In the perfect silence of that understanding I knew that my mother loved me in the very sinews of my own lovemaking.

She loved my love as her own feeling. And now she meant for me to feel her coming out like a hidden intaglio on the roughened surface of my goose-pimpling flesh.

"But I have my book..."

My first find was self-discovery. I believed in myself because of it.

I think of the ground I walked on then as a membrane to be pierced, though it was spongy with the vast compression of decayed vegetable matter, and answered the spring of my stride with its own counterstep. Peat bog felt to me a natural substance of my becoming. It was, after all, the land I had been born to and had already inherited—though the money needed to support myself upon it had wasted away with my father's poor tubercular frame—and upon which I had resolved to make my trade.

Blackman's Heath. It had already spoken of what could be discovered in the solid depths of its long absorbed bog waters. Once, in the years of my impressionable childhood, when footprints on the heath always led to a scavenger's trench, we heard tell that the local amateur archeologist, who instructed the dry-mouthed children in the village, had one day thrust his spade through the peated crust, severing an ankle and foot from a lightly buried leg. Millet Man *the specimen was unimaginatively baptized. He lay upon his sack of millet. It seemed to shine through his belly, where the arch of his back over the mound concatenated its shape in the stretch of the leather tunic that filled him out in front. His inner lip encrusted with seeds told the tale of his misery. The belly full as the sack. Force-fed with grass and with water to bloat it. Its bursting had been something which occurred quietly beneath the clothes. The trained eye could find it with a finger sensitive to the crack in an eggshell.*

It was on the basis of this discovery that our Dublin museum experts surmised the existence of a grain market within walking distance of the brutally hobbled traveler.

So years afterward, because the heath was still sodden with that surmise, I was able to persuade my financial backers that no one should know better where to look than I, the master of this particular horizon. Though the domain was mine by civil law, I swore I could be trusted to treat it as if it were already signed to the deed of history.

And with Sophia's dowry I was able to purchase a museum title of my own. So that when I etched my finger across our first view of the excavation site, to direct the official setting of perimeter stakes, I was not merely exercising a birthright. It was a privilege of the scientific method, which owed no fealty to the primogeniture that slept in my bones, as quietly as those bodies in the bog.

It was the scientist who was fully awakened to the task of discovery.

I had been to university after all. I was professionally mantled with degrees. I knew how to act.

I was a tall man then, possessing the perfect frame and carriage for the costume of the field: the pouffed jodhpurs and boots with oilskin gaiters, the khaki epaulets, the houndstooth cape, gnarled briar stick and, most impressively, the hat that was like a surveyor's instrument. A compass and barometer were mounted into the crown. The wide brim was expansively marked with the radii of latitude and longitude. From the leather chinstrap a plumb line hung to a leaden ball.

The most disparaging of my critics always said I carried the stage with me. And I am the first to admit I knew how to tred on it—with the authority of any crowned character—so as to muffle the creaking of the floorboards with the sheer weight of my bombast.

It takes as much to raise the dead, in a manner lively enough to intrigue our friendly benefactors. The museums need their audience too. The audience must be served. I have always thought of my financial backers as happy mourners. And they pay for a rite that is, in truth, a meticulous antithesis of the funeral which real bereavement never profited from. And the more inscrutable and violent the death I play out before them, the more the veil of mourning is lifted above the fluttering eyes of their titillation. So what could have pleased them more than the discovery that, what we had confidently surmised to be a grain market, was in reality a pitiless place of execution?

In my impromptu report to the local chapter of The National Archeological Society—they urged me to speak from the podium where my voice might gain the full volume of the room, might reach the backers in the back, plumed in cigar smoke and clouded with whisky, I laid the scene.

I asked them to see the march of hooded figures, wending toward the frayed perimeter of a desolated reed settlement. It is the last of the reed communities, their fishing lakes choked with infill, their huts roofless and gone to mud. The death-sentence procession, dogged by hecklers and the timid cries of the mourners-to-be sounding like mice on short tether, is led by its helpless victims into an outlying gloom.

I implored the members of the society to see a curious thing: arriving at its destination, the procession would have seemed to be taken up into a divine cloud. Victims and persecutors alike are engulfed in incensed smoke at the approach of the doomward ground. But it is an illusion. From quashy wellsprings far below them, the queasy earth—a thousand years before our feet find footing on it—continuously discharged a gaseous lake into the declivity of ground they sought. The priestly punishers descended alone with their herd of penitents.

What transpired below, the choices of dry punishment or

wet, burial alive or drowning, has been curiously reserved for our eyes only, floating to the surface of the gaseous lake these eons after the deed. But if one had waited on the bluff ground then with the hecklers and the mourners until a smaller procession returned from the hidden depths, one would have seen that the priests' hands were now free of the implements of murder. One would have tried to peer beneath the eddying mists. But one would have kept his feet on solid ground. The earth has a restless tongue when so much water collects without a swallow.

And yet I have forgotten why I am remembering this episode. Why am I writing? At this moment I am a brute creature of my book, a monster hauling itself from a mysterious deep of my own and into an atmosphere that is strangely unbreatheable.

Now I awaken from the spell of remembering, like a dreamer who turns upon one still sleeping shoulder. And when I loosen my jaws to cry out, it is as if I am the one who receives a mouthful of dirt that is packed as tightly outside me as all my squirming organs are within. My eyes are damp clods in which the images of what I can't see are the dense coagulants of darkness.

Yet, here and now, I can see that the pen is stuck in my plumped fist like an arrow into the core of an apple. The page on which I have been writing trembles like water in which the pen would serve as a laughable oar. And though I can read what I have surely just written myself, it does not rescue me from the sinking feeling.

I must continue to write. I realize it is the act of continuing that is important. If I continue, then I am, in a sense, remembering, if only the present act: the rolling entanglement of the inky letters, the perspiration shimmering on my wrist bone, the grain shining though the resinous finish of my escritoire like bones flashing through sunlit water, the warmth of the lamp glow holding everything together like a flow of hot wax. I even smell the bodily ferment of my recent discombobulation rising around me like the freshly stirred pot and I am content to rise with it.

Who would disagree that it is only by remembering the present that we can imagine the future?

Here and now I can say it calms me immeasurably to remember that the moment that is passing takes me with it, if I will go.

x x x x x

Do you think she didn't tell me what it was like to be a victim?

An old man, he is. But his is a body that only knows frailty in the thing it crushes. Cinna possessed the green eyes of my mother which—flashing emerald in the lamplight—enabled me to discern the truth of what she told.

She told me that he came down into the hole with her when she reached the level of imminent discovery. Excavation is such a curious intimacy, in any case.

Cinna lay luxuriantly in my bed when she spoke the words, as if turning the earth with her tongue, breaking a silence that had buried us both under the leaden physicality of our breath-defying exertions. Now cooling in one another's arms, we were especially sensitized to the vehement heat of the words that were flashing with her resentment.

She told me how the hole, cut to the size of one digger—slim as she was—was suddenly gorged with Dundeed's unwelcome presence. She felt like she had been forced inside him. His breathing compressed her lungs. The twist of his rotating girth pinched the trowel from her fingertips, catching up the rest of her angularity like a clutch of knuckles in loose dough. His smell bristled on her tongue. One moment she had been on hands and knees inspecting the membranous turf face that fairly pulsed the announcement of a discovery. In the next she was set on her haunches, upended the way an addition of water will straighten a stick in a bottle.

The sampling holes were dug like wellheads over the expanse of the excavation site—in a random pattern which, if the dots were connected, would I'm sure have resembled the looping mathematical signature of infinity—the better to explore the underground holdings without draining bank funds. Substantial expenditures are reserved for the full scale effacement of the gradient, requiring diesel graders and truck-bed sifters.

Once Cinna had let her excitement leap from the bottom of the hole—a premature utterance she admitted, biting the tip of her tongue into a bloody heart shape between wet, whitening teeth—the senior archeologist could not be denied his supervision. Dundeed took charge as if it were something to be yanked from her grip. He gave orders for the hole to be dilated with hand spades and a miniaturized backhoe. He oversaw the slow effacement of the gradient. He inspected the grainy pyramids of sifted backfill that held together like a bristling hive of iron filings under the spell of an invisible magnet.

Dundeed made her feel his presence amidst her breezy expectancy like a sweat, griming her joints, weighing on her clothes. She would have left handprints on the walls of her confinement if they needed lath and plaster to close her in. She squirmed to tell me this, as if we two shared the same tight space.

Then I saw that my mother's eyes were hooded with Cinna's aversion of my motherward gaze. Knowing the green resemblance was something I inveigle, like coaxing a bird from the ledge onto a tame finger, Cinna was refusing to let me see through her that way. Wrinkling the lines of her face, scribbling over the picture of my mother I made in my mind, she refused what she called my efforts to make her speak with my mother's voice. Stirring abruptly from the crook of my arm she made the next words tingle between my legs, feathering her fingertips towards my groin, as if to push the bird from the ledge.

Cinna told me how Dundeed waited until the enlarged circumference of the hole had ebbed to the level of her untimely exclamation before he opened his mouth to her. Though they stood together on an edge of time, peering past their boot tips into the bottom of the pit, she said she saw herself then as a figure forced to stand up in a draining pool, exposing to the glare of sunlight, the nudity that the water level had protected. An odd view I thought until, with a narrowing of her green eyes, she made me see Dundeed's lurid intent.

I'm sure he held her hand in his two, warming her egglike fist with the expectation that whatever fledgling life would hatch out might be instantly imprinted with his own rubbery twitch. But she told me of his smile instead. How the lips felt for the plumpness of each word before letting it go. And indeed the first words weighed against her gut like the itch to regurgitate.

Filling the hole with his shadow, while hers fell prone upon unexcavated turf, Dundeed told her this was a *hymeneal moment*: "It always is for the digger whose eyes must be peeled to the thinness of the onion, when he first senses that the merest veil of earthly covering drawn over the specimen at the bottom of the hole may in fact be the sudden shape of what was thought to be so veiled. It might be instead too transparently present to the touch. If one breaks the veil one ravages what was on the other side, since the fact that there was another side has just been proved to be the sheerest illusion." Always a speech-maker. Dundeed's voice was a mumbly sock in Cinna's mouth. Perhaps she smiled to show me she could do him so deftly.

Dundeed had a reason for telling her this. The reason was no doubt already pulsing in the grip he tightened upon her whitening fingers. She said she remembered only the wetness. Seepage from the nerve endings that she imagined could be followed back to a dense black netting fitted over his brain as tightly as a filthy sock on a sweaty foot.

When he spoke next she imagined him peeling the sock, the words gave off such a florid fetor. He begged a bargain with her. He told her he wished her to be as the earth was for him in its yielding to discovery. Would she embrace him? Would she let what was hidden within her appear to him like something sifted through sand? And would she let him preserve her earthiness as a stain upon the fingers of his passionate hand?

In exchange he promised she could have full charge of what might be—even imminently—discovered at their feet. He would yield back to her, her place in the still uncrypted earth. Hers could be the hand that touched the other side of the veil before anyone else knew that it had been drawn away.

She might even name the feeling that fitted itself to the mummified form toward which—she confessed in the most liquid tone—she was already moving.

Cinna turned away from my recumbent anatomy, the better to see what she was about to recollect, and in doing so, inadvertently drew off the bed sheet from the milky flow of her lower back and buttocks.

From the hiddenness of her face, Cinna declared that she never imagined it would be a discovery more spectacular than any she had read about in books. I may have detected a blush ripening the pear shape of her behind, rising, and flickering in the small of her back, as she completed the turn.

Then Dundeed permitted her to return to her work.

In the ground again and on her knees, she cocked her wrist, focused her eye, and lowered her head to the plane of the workspace. She told me that the first brisk strokes of her horse-hair brush seemed to gather an entanglement with the turf particles they were meant to stir into the air. Wispy ends of coarse fiber sprouted from the ground as well, as if pulled from the hasp of the brush. But what at first appeared to be the wild strands of a prodigious subterranean scalp were revealed, after the application of a wide-toothed comb and the prying blade of a penknife, to be the stiff notch of a horse's tail. It looped out of the earth like the proverbial ring of brass.

Judging from the angle of its protuberance into Cinna's view, the massive animal pendant to that tail could be envisioned falling through the earth in which, what the Field Inventory would term its "bucking action," was congealed. She surmised that if it were visible in the air through which such falling was possible, the animal would have appeared to be suspended by the pinch of godlike invisible fingers pressing the svelte withers, where one would otherwise think the animal was sucking in its breath.

Excavation of the forequarter of the specimen, to the depths of the hooves, revealed it to be a horse as red as the juice of a pomegranate. Dipped in that hue, the hairs of the hide held the paint as passionately as any artist's brush. And the mane indeed stood on end to confirm the thrashing of the enormous long head. Dangling at the bottom of the arc of the neck, it would have flung itself into the sky, as if the neck itself were a scythe whirring through air. The paint would have speckled the grim colorless faces of the fearful minions charged to keep the beast pacified in the harnesses of the ritual that began with the changing of its color. The cold scraping of Cinna's voice against that fact, digging deeper into her recollection, told me that she had known very well how the ritual had ended.

When fully unearthed and transposed from the vertical plane in which its forehoofs would have supported the double bladed kick, (snapped like a whiplash from its spine) to the horizontal plane in which the softest eyes could swim with a pacific view of its outstretched anatomy, Cinna took in every detail. Though the process had left the equine shoulders and haunches a bit rumpled, like a costume sloughed from the wobbly gait of drunken party-goers, still the wonder of its size, its shocking color, and above all the immortalized kick—the twist of the shaggy neck, the barrel roll of the under-girth evoking the lightness of air against what must have been the densest impact of dirt—drained the vision from Cinna's eyes. Her fascination soaked into every bristle of the hide.

She would know the animal from its roots. First she looked hard into the double bore of the nostrils so violently painted with the last snort of breathable air. With a cold knife edge, Cinna peeled a membrane of mud from one flared eye, exposing the pupil black itself, as a tadpole socketed in a pucker of mud. She ran her thumb along the lower mandible of the skull, wiggled her finger into the flaccidly pricked ears, counted the vertebrae like budding teeth under the coarsened hide. The paint had encrusted the hide, making it scabrous to the touch. Only the cleft of the mare's vented hindquarters ran smooth against the thrust of Cinna's bundled fingers.

The wringing of her hands over such a specimen had been so exultant that her gloves bled with the horse's hue.

When I thought the spade turned in her recollection of the event, Cinna's face turned back to me, the green glimmer of my mother's eyes still shining through the murk of her expression. The furrowed brow, the apparent jostle of the cheekbones under the tight fit of the skin, the disgusted roll of the under lip might have been a disfiguring spadeful of earth cast over my mother's patient gaze. But its look came through as undying as ever. I tell you I didn't just see it in Cinna's face. She showed it to me.

There are faces buried in faces, the dead awakened in their tombs. Most of the time Cinna harbored her unwelcome ghost out of love for me, however harrowing her resentful moods threatened to become. Like any woman, she loved the love of the good son in me, despite her unwillingness to suckle the mother's likeness for my greedy gaze.

But her protest this time was not against my recognition that she looked out of my mother's eyes. It battled against what she had left to say of Dundeed's unconsummated crime. I could see the telling of it caught in her throat, a grudging tumescence that pressed her lips into a surly kiss.

When Cinna had declared the last fact of her forensic brief with a click in her mouth as silvery as the latch of the physician's treatment case, she stepped away from the equine specimen, which now lay at her feet like a trophy rug.

As if it lay triumphantly across the parquet of his own library floor, Dundeed stepped forward with all the authority of an arresting policeman. Silently, he knelt between the stiffly sprung legs, pointed and then drew his finger along an invisible meridianal seam that had been hidden from view in the crisp shrivel of the skin reticulating upon the distended belly. He cleared his throat.

Like a fine hatch work of shadow in a yellowed engraving, the stitching along the seam revealed what lay in its concealment. An incision had been cut from the draft to the withers, the length of which was sufficient to accommodate the removal of every internal organ, not to mention the reach of hairy forearm that would have been needed for thieving hands to go to the depths of the cavity.

But the breadth of the wound, which opened its lips to the most vivid imaginings of the ritual of removal, did not even hint at what had been just as ritualistically placed within the empty cavity. The blade that was secreted in the straightness of Dundeed's instructive finger, as he drew it a second time along the length of the suture, was the ultimate revelation. What had itself been buried for nine hundred years had been devised to be the burial chamber for what one would never have imagined could be contained within it.

An elbow flapped loose from the gaping pouch of the equine belly, as if whatever was inside might be fledgling and alive. But as Dundeed inserted a latex-gloved finger where the blade had glided along one edge of the opened seam, Cinna understood what was to be seen if one stooped to Dundeed's crouching level: what had seemed to her to be evidence of the animal's helpless bucking against the covering earth—because the horse had been buried alive—was only evidence that, in its sinking into a prehistoric mire, it had been unbalanced by the weight of its own no less struggling cargo: a man alive, sewn up into the belly of a horse.

The full exposure of the cavity, still dependent upon the pressure of Dundeed's probing fingertip, revealed the already small figure, brown and loin-clothed, mercilessly hunched into conformity with his confinement. Nevertheless the death rigor seemed to be sprung inside him, giving the appearance of a sculpted figure struggling to escape the stone. The fingers laced through the horse's rib cage, the back humping against the spine, even the naked buttocks gaining leverage against the bony heels, were all the force needed to explain the illusion that the horse had been frantically in motion in the depths of its burial.

The blue face that seemed to be tattooed onto the skull, grinning at her, turned upside down as it was, and staring at her from under the elbow that had first flung the sight of him into her startled view. That unhappy grin, so gristled there upon his lips, conveyed the bitter taste of Cinna's humiliation, as if she had knelt hard against Dundeed's still stooping form and kissed them herself.

Instead, she stood apart and immobilized in the speechlessness of her mistaken hypothesis, like an animal contemplating the leg that must be gnawed off before it can be free from the jaws of the sprung trap.

In the enthusiasm of her discovering a horse, buried where no scholar believed the species had ever trod above ground, she had failed to discover the more uncommon thing: a man, buried inside a horse. Dundeed had taken the triumph of her first discovery and still held entitlement to his discovery of her.

You ask me how I know she was telling the truth and I remind you that I was her lover *after* he was my teacher. Who better to corroborate the deed than the one who has inducted the methods of the perpetrator?

Good as her word, Cinna went to Dundeed that night with a weight of earth accumulating in her stride—hips and legs working like tired shoulders into a stoop—as if she could bury the knowledge of what she was about to do before she would find herself in the midst of its own laborious physicality. She recollected to herself that for this promise she had lowered herself into a hole. For the right to become herself, she had given away her person. When she had stepped down, she had even been contented to know that she no longer possessed what merely filled the space.

Now, anticipating the old man's weight (he tumesces in so much of his skin, it is hard to imagine him having the reserves he would need even for that ragged scrap hanging between his legs), she felt the space around her like a torrid smear.

Dundeed had requested her to come to his library step. Not his bedroom. Not his office. I'm imagining his expectation piqued by the sting of the binding molds, stitching their rankness to the lining of his nose. There he waits, strangling a sneeze in one nostril, flattening himself behind the glass paneled door to the library, his eye fattening with its attention to the impenetrable darkness without.

Cinna turned the emerald green mirror of my mother's eye upon me to tell me what I can make you see now, because I am alive to say it and she is not. Do you miss her as much as I?

When she thought to herself that he was indeed inside her (a man enfolded in so much flesh will have difficulty finding the outer edge of himself) she knew he was there for destruction. She smelled a clod of dirt on his breath, felt the impress of him like a glottal catch in her throat, heard the phlegm dislodged from the branching tubes in his lungs, like apples shaken from a stormblown tree, when the spasm of his entry caught up with the blind purposiveness of his thrusting. Then, surprised as she was to discover she still had a grip that could be broken, Cinna had the ineliminable sensation that something was tearing away from her.

It was in fact herself that fluttered like the shred of a thing torn loose. And yet the tremors were the pulse of her certainty that she still had blood to spill. If she were to have judged by the tremors alone, she would have believed a man was galloping insider her. But the blows would seem to have fallen on the outside of her body, a fact which you could know if you had consulted the register of hospital reports and in particular the case of a woman who officially protested that she had been thrown by a horse. No name given. I'm sure you'll find it a brimming well of suspicion.

This despite the attending physician's unflinching observations that the blood clouding her skin silhouetted the grip of a large and powerful hand. The blush in her cheek was legible with the crisp lettering of an insignia ring. And the horse that was said to have thrown her had more likely ridden her, if the truth could be said to flow from the evidence of internal hemorrhage, not to mention the appalling displacement of those organs that otherwise benignly kiss the uterus even amidst most energetic motions of the pelvis.

Because neither do the hospital documents flinch from the blows he felled upon her, I urge you to read them yourself. Open your eye before he opens his maw. Form the picture in your mind and hold fast to it before the gong stroke of Dundeed's speech makes the facts sound a different story.

I can already hear him lyricizing the violence, inviting us to think that sexual roughness is an appetite, a kind of connoisseurship. The black and blue body is well fed with the blood of its most fervent desire.

Or, knowing his need to allude to the faultiness of his memory—how else would he remember it?—he will ask you to help him. He will ask you for the back of your ring-adorned hand. Slap him. He will implore you. "Slap me!" See if the blow summons any incriminating knowledge, by its unthinking likeness to the alleged assault. See what knowledge concatenates then.

And your slap *will* remind him. But only because he chooses to dilate upon the warmth of the afterblow (and not the force of the blow itself) which he will tell you resembles nothing so much as the warmth of Cinna's side when she slept peacefully beside him. He will repeat that she slept beside him, uttering those words no farther from your face than you stand yourself when you are leaning into the gravitational field of his "innocent" testimony, to check the look in his eyes.

Lean closer. He will say it is her smell that he recognizes on your breath, as if you were the cat who had eaten the canary. He might even flatter you. He might even remark upon a resemblance to the curve of her buttocks in the tensed curvature of your bending back when, bending deeper into his shadow, you realize that the eyes you are peering into would do as well in the head of a dead bird to tell you what lurks beyond the light, shining like shoe gloss, upon their surfaces.

x x x x x

FIELD INVENTORY: (October 11, 1975) Specimen #3, Crate #6

Elderly male. 1 meter, 22 centimeters. Left leg measures 17.78 centimeters shorter than its partner. Legs twisted astride of what is assumed to be a briar walking stick. Arms crossed over the chest and tied at the wrists into a self-embrace. Wrists lashed around neck with a coarse linen twine. A jute mesh bag also hangs around the neck to waist level, where it has clearly engaged the hips in the body's struggle for air.

Contents of the jute bag: three human heads. Young boys, between the ages of ten and fifteen. The three scalps have been knotted together. The eyes of all three are open. But mineral replacements have left them indistinguishable in color and texture from other fleshy parts, the lips and nose, the high-boned cheeks.

NOTATION: the autopsy reports that the enamel of the outer fascia on the elder's upper right incisor is etched with hatch marks in a longitudinal sequence. The count goes to three.

It is not only because he claims to possess a good memory that I accuse him of dwelling unhealthily in the past. He does wrong to her memory precisely as he did wrong to her person, by indulging his fetish for likenesses.

Surely you know how far *like* is from *love* when those two become lost to one another in the forest of desire. The lover who is titillated by likenesses deserves to become the victim of the princess who transforms herself into a witch. But, invariably the lover of likenesses himself is the one who wields the most monstrous capability.

Our Taste's for his mother. We know that already. And we know from his own account how Cinna bridled under the eye of the loving son when he fastened it upon her like a cinched strap. That he saw Cinna in the image of the woman who had brought him into the world, already bespeaks the most regressive urges, does it not? It means that he would have had little tolerance for the felt texture of that tender woman's own experience. His every gesture towards her was covetously inclined to take something away. He never shared the *here and now* with her. And therefore he can make no claim of knowledge that might seriously assert superiority over my own: limned as it is in the radiantly flushed palpability of the immediate moment.

This Taste has already drawn the titillating lash of his violent imagery over the quivering skin of your imagination. He is hoping to enflame your whole being against me, welting your indignation, until the pains he says she suffered under my fevered hand migrate from your head into the joints and extremities of your writhing frame.

Let me however assure you there is a subtler and more malicious violence enacted in touching the focal point of one's own sharp eye to another's face and cutting the silhouette of what one wishes to see: cutting out the light by which one would otherwise see what is actually there.

See him do it. She would have been your height to him, though her hair fell to her hips when she loosened it. Your hips shoulder the weight of your torso with the same tottering dance step that gave her locomotion. If you bumped me now I might be able to tell you what she weighed, my sensitivity to the present moment is so strong. Be bold enough to let the weight of your own body drop from your hipbone into the willing support of my open palm, and I may be able to remind you that her athleticism had density as well as litheness. See her with the clarity of your own body.

Will you not? Is squeamishness a little-known trick of the investigative trade? I wouldn't have thought so.

But see her only to imagine how he must have harmed her by his look. You've heard him describe the mother. I don't remember. But I can imagine the struggle under the skin that he must have fomented with his first kiss. Can you see how he holds Cinna's head between his hands, the knuckles gleaming, how his eyes bore in?

What you can't see, unless I continue, is that in her hand, curved behind her back, Cinna clutches five gleaming fingernails, enameled tulip red, red as the lips he told her his mother never had need to color. What you can't see is that the two of them are standing in heaps of their sloughed clothing, their heads shadowed upon the mildewed beams that shore up my Sanctuarium Scholasticus—private as the tomb it has been—and that she is daring him to see her for the woman his mother was not.

But his eyes are now glazed. Perhaps in them she catches the shine of one of my early discoveries reflecting from its frame on the near wall. He perches his hands on her shoulders. He steps out of the well of his fallen belt and trousers and plants both feet apart on the brick floor. His calves are shaking. They appear to be immersed in flowing water. His arms, in the swiftest part of that current, flow around her waist.

You can read the words "Hold still" on his lips, but there is only the sound of the soles of her feet slapping the floor. I have never challenged his boasts of physical prowess. Here he is lifting her up and letting her fall. He is showing her *her* weight in the muscular heave of his upper arms.

I could show you yours if you would lend your physical self more selflessly to my account.

But isn't it clear that he is *not* innocently lifting her up and letting her down, as if in prelude to some acrobatic defiance of gravity designed to make the spectator's heart rise, on a silver string of tension, into the beautiful constrictions of a velvet throat. No. He is only making her face pass before his eyes. Not in the way of looking to see her rise or fall, but looking for the rhythm of his mother's eyes—as he remembers it when she rocked him in her arms, when, though he was in greater motion than she, he found the stillness upon which he would now impale Cinna's heart.

We have spoken of regressive urges! Now he does impale her upon the florid arousal sprouting between his legs, that is more like the weathered horn of a hoary goat facing starvation on an unleapable mountain ledge, than the twist of muscle stitched too tightly into the skin. I only extrapolate to such remote regions of feeling to make you know how his own penchant for likenesses was as remote an exile of her feeling from its fondness.

At the instant he lifts her this time, to toggle her anatomy to the spark of his ardor, his eyes close. Roscoe Taste is now in the mausoleum of his mother's memory. It is fittingly womblike to his most dangerous thoughts about the woman whose living body is, at the same moment, incubating his most ecstatic yearnings, and is herself utterly unaware of what monstrosity can be born from such morbid humidity. With his hands gripping the backs of Cinna's thighs he is feeling his way along a mausoleum wall. The dark wall is leaking into his grip: condensation beading from the membranous contact of this passionate moment with the marble chill that makes the mausoleum his own pursuit. You can hear her cries, but they do not echo in the mausoleum halls.

Can you not imagine what I am telling you? Does it defy the squint of your worst suspicions? But why shouldn't you be prepared to witness what you surely should have envisioned yourself upon hearing him speak too fervently of his maternal devotion? Yes I remember because I heard it, like you, only brief moments ago. It is no miracle and I am no liar. I admit my recollection fades. But over time. Over time. And like the cooling glow of a tungsten filament it is enlightening to the end.

Doesn't memory serve *you* well? Did he not tell us that his mother's body was a crypt for his most morbid desire? Didn't we hear how his mind is sung to the sound of his mother's keening? She cradled his naked body in her arms when he was large enough to shed an odor where he lay.

His mother loved him "in the sinews of his lovemaking." Didn't he say so himself? His words, you'll recall, have the effect of making us see things that we ought not to titillate with our eyes. And yet, in confessing his mother's passion for his own most flushed exertions in the arms of a fawn and moody girl, he gives us a glimpse of the hunchback—with beauty slung over one shoulder—scurrying along the tunneled passageways of the mausoleum.

A specter that puts our dread in hot pursuit. Does it not?

Do we follow? Do we hearken after splashing footsteps and the stifling whiff of the oil lamp? The camel shadow galloping into the darkness ahead of us? Don't we know that within the walls of the mausoleum we are lost? We already know that the labyrinth of tunnels is only solved by the insight—like the thread slipped from the eye of the needle—that one will never arrive at the treasured room or even be able to trace one's steps back to the open air, which leaks from the breathless pace of one's panic as one realizes it.

But what I am saying is simple. Why do you make me out to be so obliquely obtuse, as if you yourself were the mandarin over-interpreter of my plain and robust speaking?

I am simply telling you that a man who dwells in the past can be a danger and a harm to those who breathe the air of the here and now. Like a clot of dirt in the windpipe.

Here and now I can say it with the authority of a memoryless mind.

And can you not hear the gurgle in her breath? In his arms she is in his mother's grip. She is in the bowels of the mausoleum where every touch is deathly. The fingers wriggling out of the dirt are worms in the fruit of her happiness. When he breaks it open like the fervid cleft of a peach, in the sun-drenched moment of its ripening, you would expect him to eat the worms.

Would you not? Can you not begin to see how his motive is formed? Can you not see, with the simplicity of my unflinching eye, that he has tasted her intractability in the kiss that brought her to embrace him here? He has not mistaken the gleam of the fingernails she has tattooed on the bulky pulse of his bicep, outshining the fever of his own blood. He has sensed that Cinna will not be a host to his parasitic fancy. He knows her skin crawls at the cold touch of the mausoleum. She will not be held captive by the damp claw of its architecture. She will force doors open to the undulating air without. She will make the stones fall on his head. Unless he acts.

Can you not see then, how the hand that grasps her thigh just beneath the crease of the buttock, though it is companion to her passionate grip on his upper arm, might well be weighed upon by the temptation to use what force of his hips she trusts to consummate her pleasure, instead to drive her head into the waiting wall?

Do you imagine that a man who dwells so passionately in the past would not find it natural to let his passion be the instrument of his obsession? Do my words not prickle like the hairs rising on the back of your neck? They remember, in the tensile alertness of their horror, that the victim's head bore the tooth of a sharp blow. No one thinks of the wall as a voracious beast, I know. But even a wall can be goaded to bite, by a vicious hand.

Pore your eye, like a full magnifying glass, over the forensic blow ups—why do you call them that?—of the fatal wound. Submit to the chill of the forensic lab, the deathly touch of the metal chair. Scour the evidence more patiently. The photographs might indeed spark an explosion under your scalp to show you how much the whitening split in the skull looks like nothing so much as a crack in the wall we speak of.

Though the victim was discovered in a muddy trough, a ravine intended to drain the excavation site, and though the head was bruised all over, though especially upon the crown of the skull, it is not unimaginable that she was killed in a low ceiling chamber conceived for burial, with beamed ceiling, earthen floor, and plastered walls, which show a trace of the crime no more conspicuous than the apparent smudge of a bug where it met the lifeline of a furious palm.

× × × × ×

Would I kill my own gestating offspring? If I am so immaturely a child of motherhood myself, as Professor Dundeed contends, would I have a heavy enough hand to raise against the child?

I have told you that there is a mirror for my motive, no bigger than a fingernail clipping—precisely the image you may remember—which clings, more perilously than ever, to the wall of Cinna's uterus. Look there with your most magnifying laboratory eye.

Think a moment. If we are to believe that I wished only to excavate the bones of my mother from the flesh of Cinna's passionate embrace, does it not follow that my dementia would achieve its most potent consummation by physically inseminating her with the idea she refused to bear of her own psychic volition? I ask you. Is there a better resemblance to mother than motherhood itself? Is there better corroboration of the facts I set before you?

Cinna did not hide the fact. She was already spying on her own body for signs of the semblance to pregnant womanhood.

And is it not true that the blood of a newly pregnant woman comes to the surface of the skin, as if to drink the sunlight of its tomorrow? She traced its tidemark on the places of her body where a woman's blood is ordinarily the most agitated. In the mirror she followed spidery reaches of blue pigment where the legs join the torso, where the breasts heave against the flushed skin of the throat. She held a vigilant eye for the first signs of swelling, expectant as anyone trained to wait for things that come startling out of flat ground.

And don't you know, under the spell of pregnancy, Cinna let her resentment of my mother's likeness—whether she conceded that she wore it or no—ebb, as the flow of her own motherhood carried her off on a current of swifter resemblances than even she could navigate by the lights of her own reckoning.

And what do you think? Her embrace became more motherly. My head nesting in the cradle box of her rocking arms, felt her ever more tender touch as a growing appreciation of the resemblances which I maintain love divines: making way for what yearns to pass between us. Would it be perverse to speculate that what the son sees in the mother, the mother-to-be sees in the fathering son? Was Cinna finally using my eyes to dilate her heart?

When I stepped down into the low and darkly humid chamber that Dundeed had confabulated into his mockery of a scholar's Sanctuarium Scholasticus, I expected light from Cinna's smile to welcome my footsteps. The place where Dundeed staged his likeness to the bookish scholar whom his person had no patience to be was, for that reason, a place of assignation where we assumed we would never be intruded upon by his bulking presence. What I didn't expect was the news that Cinna's lightest countenance smiled upon that day.

A child, she announced.

"Your child," she said it would be. For a moment the words rang out of a hollowness of my comprehension, as if she meant her presence would not be required at its birth. I saw this could not have been her meaning, as soon as she took my hand and placed it on what she called the little mound of her motherhood. One touch and what rounded the hollowness of

my incomprehension warmed into substance, like the breath of a whispered intimacy in the basin of a reddening ear.

Warmth and wetness. They were the elements of the moment in that low and dimly ovoid space where the decor of Dundeed's abandoned retreat—the walnut escritoire bearing water spots like a disease of the skin, the leather armchair sprouting the hair of an almost animalcular fungus, the oil lamp rigged from the support of a section of reconstructed vertebrae raising its phantom posture from a leaden base—all began to swirl in the emotional flood that nearly swept me off my own feet. I was so moved.

"It will be your child," she repeated, as if *she* were the inseminator of the idea. For me it was still a buoyant object in the high water of my affection, eluding my grip as I lunged after it and in doing so risked an unsettling flotation myself. The reaching after it made the question pop up like a sudden air bubble in my throat, "What do you mean?"

"You know that I'll leave you with it. You'll have it alone—as if *you* were the mother who, as you also know, cannot share the experience of birth nor the child itself, without absenting herself. What else does a womb do but shuck itself of the squirming fruit?"

By now she held my face in her hands. I could feel my flushed cheeks ruffling above her grip on my chin like wings over a freshly dropped egg.

"No, I don't intend to die in childbirth," she said, without equivocation, smiling, batting her eyelashes. "I intend something even more absent, and so more resonant for you."

But that was her last word. Everything that followed was in pantomime, narrated only by her breathing. It heaved from her broad chest like bags of cement being hefted into waiting arms.

Dropping to the floor like one of the sacks herself, she made me understand that I was standing upon what she wished to disclose.

The sharp tug on the cuff of my trouser leg coaxed my boot into a clumsy dance step, over the coarsely hemmed border of the canvas drop cloth, which served for carpeting over the fibrous turf floor. A deft jerking of the canvas revealed the peat beneath it, cut into four bricks and marked out as a larger square, against the otherwise flat contour of the earth. She needed the fingers of both hands to prise each brick from its nest. The sucking sound that respired from the first removal filled my mouth with the impulse to speak. But she thrust a finger in front of her own lips with such vehemence that I had to bite my tongue. Her eyes were already below ground. The slope of her shoulders and lower back, where she dipped head and arms into the vaultlike space of the excavation, made my thoughts slip upon the moment of breathless silence that followed.

"Something...more resonant for you," I thought I heard her say again, even though she lifted her treasure from the vault in a gesture of sobriety, so smugly soundless, that her lips seemed as pinched against any expulsion of air as the pink tail of a balloon.

Because she cradled it as if it were alive, I didn't realize until I took it from her that the bundle was as cold and damp as a refrigerated kidney. But, had it been throbbing with heat, it would have been no easier to see that, what appeared to be the tarry butt-end a turf log was, upon closer inspection, an infant face. The nose and chin pressed back into the gray mud of the skull had more the aspect of a footprint than any human expression that might have called out to a squinting curiosity. And, of course, I recognized it immediately as a member of Dundeed's "sleeping family." That was how Dundeed honored his finds from the site, that we all understood had never been a grain market as the first archeological maps surmised, but was always a place where punishment was meted out in the suffocating depths of a bubbling black mire. Always a place of punishment. And from it now a baby had been born. But what was she telling me?

Was she not recalling us to Dundeed's own account of the catastrophic marriage ceremony that left him bereft of a bride, but by no means, childless? Has he not corroborated, in his absurdly operatic tale of that grief—down to the details of a birth that mocks even the mockery of credulity—the existence of what Cinna placed in my arms that day? Of course Dundeed could not have known what he was saying then, since he had not yet heard what I am telling you here and now. But here and now we both know how to wonder if the skills of the archeologist are not too well suited to disguising as a relic the crime of the moment. Now we know how to wonder that the woman had reason to hate him. Sophia Pasthand indeed! Now we know how to wonder that the woman had reason to leave him. We shall never know what happened.

But, now we know how to wonder that it did.

Now I see that, in revealing to me Dundeed's secret, Cinna meant to show us what we contend with when we attempt to sift the wheat from the chaff with this dissembling merchant of phantom grain. Cinna speaks to us. The resonance is unmistakable. Could this be what she meant when Cinna promised something "more resonant" for me? Could she have anticipated her own brutal end and so bequeathed this clue to those who might be someday duty-bound to do her justice? The tragedy is that her absence makes it so. And does this not prove that she never had the intention to leave me in the first place? Though she is gone, it is more accurate to say she has been taken from us. By what hand plucked from our company?

Who more entitled to ask the question than the one to whom she was most attached? Fastened by blood, I think I may now say with decency. Who more violently feels the tearing of that ligament?

× × × × ×

But I have my book.

My book remembers what I have forgotten.

I was a child myself when I recognized the strangely mirrory features of my first find. Is it any wonder that to this day no one knows of that discovery but myself?

A child exploring in shallow bog water. I was already heir to the estate at the age of fourteen. A familiar of the heath as well as its new heir. And yet, I was taken by as much surprise as any perfect stranger to learn that the ground gives issue to children of its own.

What child would have expected to see his own face where his foot had been?

Standing amid the deep crenellations of the peat, left after the attack of my gardener's spade, I turned my cheek to the wind, like the last survivor of an embattled tower. I surveyed what I now thought looked like the head of a Tyrannosaurus chewing its way out of the earth, snapping jaws come vengefully alive to my clattering footsteps—I was a heavy child, even then. What else had I been digging for?

I only knew to look for dinosaurs. A schoolbook had pictured the scientific team, standing like the ungainly children they had become beneath a skeletal articulation of ferocity. Aroused to stand upon its hind legs, it had been erected to a height of twenty-seven meters. Its reptile head seemed as lost to the outrageous scale as the woolen-vested and hobnail-booted men who posed soberly between its legs.

Now, though I wished for largeness, I noticed something just as inversely small where one of the ragged toothed imprints of my own boot-heel began to collect an oily liquid. The juice of the pulpy turf formed a taut skin of iridescence over the surface. It imparted a porcelain pallor to the shape of a cheekbone that suddenly seemed to turn toward the reflecting light from the bottom of the boot print. As I screened the sun with my stooping inspection, the oily water went as limpid as the surface of a mirror when the silver backing has eroded. So my hand was unexpectedly wet with the first touch of it. But the clarity of such a cold touch was abruptly blurred by the texture of wet tobacco leaves that seemed to be bundled into the shape of a small torso, the lower portion of the anatomy feathering away like the worn end of a straw broom, or the mouth-watered end of the cigar itself. Light as sheaved grass when I lifted it.

And yet I didn't know what I was holding until I saw my thumb come loose from what was suddenly clearly an eye socket. A round clot of plant matter smeared the white of my thumbnail like the displaced and terribly dilated pupil. A child. But so much smaller than myself. What I had never seen was an infant, though I knew the name for it as soon as I turned it over in my palms. My hands were working to make sense of what simultaneously loosened their grip upon it—out of fear or respect for what they knew they had no right to possess. And yet, the human "look" of it wouldn't lie still under the pressure of the fingers feeling only the coarsest sensation of crushed root matter, a damp humus compacted with the scent of leaves fallen centuries before, nothing even of a once soft skin soaked for a lifetime in brine.

So, in my hands, the human features were there and not there, like the very thing the eye blinks against, when it struggles to reclaim its vision from an irritant that lodges ever more blindingly in the watering muscle. The shapes of arms and legs molted from the feathery texture of the turf log and then flew black again into the shape-defying density of carboniferous plant matter. Nose and lips became distinct under eyes peering close enough to smell the dirty finger of human contact. Then, just as alarmingly, the depth of the mind's probings reverted to the surface of the earth and the appearance of a tarry clod returned. As if it were physically squirming against my recognition, I clutched it forcefully against my breast. I stilled my mind with the thought that if it had a human form that would hold, it would be my discovery. My discovery. A find!

After all, the archeological vocation was already dreaming me so vibrantly; I might have precipitously awakened to a less colorful self. But I slept on. I sleep on.

From that day, I kept the specimen in a hempen sack and never looked again, the better not to disturb such potent sleep. Whether an infant bundled in the preservative elements of natural decay or a clot of unwitting turf inadvertently cut to shape a human suggestion, the ambiguity of what I cradled in my arms that day has in no way confused the direction of my life and career. Ever since I have been on the path of the same watery boot print which caught my eye upon the ground that day and from which book I have never struggled to be free.

I am still the hooked fish.

I think of it now that I read it from my book and remember that we were only just speaking of a child, an infant specimen of dubious provenance. Do you remember?

Do you remember that this Taste wants you to imagine the unrecognizable child in Cinna's womb to have been his own? He wants you to imagine that I am only the bearer of death. Hers as well as my own.

It is impossible that one so old could fertilize such youth. He wants you to imagine the seed curdled in my loins. Think of the milk corked inside my manhood, and left for all the years that have wrinkled me, in the cobwebbed cupboard of my trouser leg. So he invites you to use your imagination.

Yes. Use your imagination. But use it more shrewdly.

Why should you heed the advisings of a man with a shambling mind, as you yourself put it?

Wasn't it I who first dared you to examine the uterus for a trace of cellular atavism no bigger than a fingernail? Now I remind you because, if you scrape that specimen onto your microscope slide, you are bound to discover that the fingerprint, so indelibly marked on the lattice grid of its cell structure, is inimitably my own. You will spy me there where the eyepiece of your microscope has your pupil dilated and swimming in incredulity.

But since the thought of one infant, so much like the thought of another, has so felicitously blown upon the coals of my memory in this flickering moment of lucidity—they are not so infrequent—let me offer you this chance to let the empty palms of your investigator's hands be warmed by a more than glowing truth. Let me offer you another reason to believe what I say, since

Cinna's child was mine long before this Taste let his thoughts slither about it, the better for his tongue to know which way to wiggle when it weaves its lies. For this Taste has let his tongue be tied in knots of contradiction.

Haven't you listened?

Am I not fat as the elephant's dying breath? A weight beyond carrying on two legs? Am I not old to the point of suppuration, my girth bursting through the worn exterior fabric of my physique, threads popping and unraveling more hectically with every frantic movement of my hands to cover the gaping holes, to pinch the seams together? Am I not weak as water and even more certainly infertile as a desert dune where nothing will flow again however wavelike the taunting motions of the parchment wind? This Taste has called me so: fat, old, weak, infertile.

Has he not?

How then does he also tell it that I am capable of abuse? A human truncheon I would be by his account. The muscles would have to stiffen considerably in the loose sleeves of my skin, wouldn't you think? And he reminds us that the corpse had to be dragged with its weight of pooled blood into the rotted gully, two hundred meters from the find site. You would need arms not so sunken in the fat of the upper body and legs that could punch the ground in a more virile stride to perpetrate the crime he accuses me of. You would need a back full of thrust and a chest full of wind to be capable of the dragging, not to mention the more finely coordinated exertions of the murderer *in the act.*

And yet, possessed of such powers—if indeed I were—wouldn't I begin to resemble the very figure of fitness who would be more than robust enough to father a child upon the most vibrant loins?

Far from self-incrimination, the resemblance I am showing you, between the fisted abuser and the athlete of virility, helps you to comprehend how similarly violent this Taste's motives would be, to the ones he accuses me of harboring against the women who loved me back. For it is still my oath. Love me, she did. And if you could believe for a moment that my physical being were indeed lively enough to wiggle its tail inside of her, wouldn't he be carrying the seed of jealousy himself? If I could be the father, as I say I am, wouldn't Roscoe Taste have to worry that he was not the man?

And remember this. Carried to full term the spiteful seed issues in a monstrous birth. I tell you, motivation springs eternal in the tortured soul. I only ask you to consider the evidence. Then your imagination is free to contend with the most elusive truth.

I ask you. Does the portent of a newborn's face conceivably stand out in these slack-lidded eyes, this nose like melted wax itself, the cheeks that have buried any semblance of bone structure, the dribbled chin, all the amorphousness that age confers upon this feral physiognomy?

Think of this. Limber as I am, I can be so light afoot that silent trespass upon the most secret vaults of another's hidden life is my own most furtive *métier*.

Who leads a more vaulted existence than Kraft Dundeed himself? Think of him seated in his chamber, straining to move from under his own weight. He, who has grown so fat, is a dank and unvisited dungeon unto himself. Then see him amid his cobwebs and ask yourself how much his is the life of the flowing body and how much is the life of the stagnating mind?

I'll tell you what I saw from out of the spyglass of my silent step. Dundeed's Sanctuarium Scholasticus is by no means sacred. I'll tell you what I saw.

He sat still, but not alone. His naked back showed the weight of what he carries before him, in corded stretch marks that lashed into the soft flesh, sagging beneath his shoulder blades. The rocking motion of such a body you might well imagine forced the leather ottoman to emit the creakings of ship's hold. But they were dwarfed by the groans that seemed to becloud the head in Dundeed's hands. What was he bemoaning, my ever more delicate footstep implored?

He sat amidst his scholarly décor. His credentials and photo memorabilia glittered like flattering eyes in the shadowed cave space. His desk was piled with dossiers. The bookshelves stood rigidified with the mildewed shelf weight of their unopened tomes. The specimen boxes perched on the loftiest shelves shed an aura of haunting daylight from the bone fragments collected within them, like cones of ash still phosphorescent from some spectacular incineration. A crimson curtain disguised the access to a crude latrine.

The only prop that was not laboriously intended to set the scene of scholarly retreat was the full-length mirror mounted opposite the escritoire. And as I passed across the squinting aperture of the half opened doorway that revealed it, the mirror showed me what I could not see from my own spectatorial vantage. He was not moaning inconsolably, but speaking to himself. The head in hand was not forsaken there, but deliberately positioned the better to address its audience.

Like a doubly deluded narcissus—doubled in size at least—Dundeed was speaking into the shadow pool of his naked lap. His shoulders, bent toward their reflection, seemed to tremble as any watery surface. Now I realized that it was the odd solicitude of the voice that I had mistaken for moaning.

Purring from the back of his throat, Dundeed was cajoling a treed cat from its fearful perch. Or alternatively, his voice as faintly redolent with speech as a piece of cheese waved in front of a knothole, he was cajoling a mouse from its invisible crouch.

The success of this entreaty was more startling than my most outrageous fancy of what he sought to arouse. For, whatever it was, it spoke back to him. A small voice, neither cat nor mouse. Answering like a voice over an empty expanse of water, the voice was clearly soliciting the hand that hung slackly over the arm of an adjacent chair. The fingers of Dundeed's hand now twitched to the sound of a word that was so furred with tenderness it could only have been a pet name, though as shy of my hearing as the cat or the mouse.

Daring to let my own head venture further forward into the space of hearing, my eyes were suddenly caught upon the sound I harried. I peered through the openings of my ears as if through crannying tunnels of my brain.

She was there in a blink of my eyes, like a cinder shed upon your fingertip from a blurring tear. My eyes bulged past my ears.

It was Cinna, crouched naked and shivering in a dark corner of the room, almost six feet apart from Dundeed's hulking form. Barely visible to my first glance, her head appeared to be stuck upon the pike length of her slender legs, which she had drawn up under her chin. Her hair curtained her face, downcast as it was, no doubt the better to miniaturize the voice. But her elbows were winging about her head in a frantic effort to stopper her ears against the low throttle of her tongue. Pushing the open palms of her hands flatter and flatter against the sides of her head, she seemed to be bent upon crushing it. She did not want to hear herself speaking?

Nor anything else I realized.

My own head swiveled between the violent folds of darkness agitating the corner of the room where Cinna squatted, and the opacity darkly concentrated into the back of Dundeed's bowing cranium. Because that opacity had teased me a step closer to gain a clearer view over Dundeed's shoulder, it caused me to feel that I myself might even be the bearer of the sound that seemed to emanate from both places at once, when it spoke again.

"You know me," it whispered into the encircling palm of his hand. He had brought the hand forward as if to guard a flickering flame. But he didn't touch himself. As puddled as the flesh appeared to be in his lap, it held only his gaze.

The voice repeated, "You know me."

And though I sensed the parted lips through which those words were emitted, as a rent in the darkness where Cinna struggled to speak, it was the sound of his words in answer that kissed the palpability of that sense.

"I know."

She had thrown her voice and he had caught it. Cinna was speaking through him and he was talking back.

Then the question of what they were speaking about was answered in the breathy buoyancy of the flesh that her voice had filled. The prayerful demeanor of his bowed head seemed veritably ensouled by the sight of himself rising from the narcissus pool, shedding its flaccidity like ecstatic tears from a fountainhead.

"Be myself again." These words were unmistakably trembled from the bristly under-jowl, just visible beneath his right ear. It stilled my foot to see the ear redden, in anticipation of the words he awaited from the darker corner of the room. Was not the red of his earlobe the first blush of the redness her voice was forcing to flower between his legs?

"I am you. I am here. I am here for you."

Three solemn declarations that raised him higher in his own eye betrayed no movement of his own body, as did his reply.

"I accept you." The motion of his own lips reticulated the folds of fat scaling the back of his thick neck. What puppet string tangled her voice with his anatomy in such an ardent manner, you can only imagine I am sure.

Only think to see his erect passion, like a painted marionette, jerked alive on the chords of Cinna's voice and you will know what I saw to have been the proof of his infertility. Doesn't every puppet have a wooden head?

So let's agree that procreation is out of the question for him who has to look for his manhood in the throat of a woman. Aren't we talking of a man whose only access to a woman's body is the exorted engorgement of her breath?

The knowing vulgarity of your smile compels me to remind you that what I am describing is the farthest thing from the lewd tickle of a sexual joke. I show you a man who, I am the first to admit, knows the raiment of human suffering. Suffice to say he is little enough of a man, let alone the capable sperm. His is a body that lives vicariously on the lips of a woman's good grace. Imagine with what anguish he had to await the acrobatic compliance of Cinna's voice! And what if the word had not been made flesh?

But what of the woman's pain? Can we guess what brutish coercion might have so cornered her in the shadows of that room? What unnatural compunction gurgles her voice into lascivious complicity with the fat man's most offending organ? As if his hands were throttling her neck instead of the thin gristle of his own lechery. What hold had he upon her pulse that made her beat her heart for him in such synchronous agony?

To see her nakedness seethe in the skein of shadows like a netted fish—though her voice was as calmly perseverant as the white lipped pucker that smothers the fish's existence in a sea of air—was to know Dundeed's most venal self, the self that had bargained her, at what unspeakable price, into this repugnant transaction of ventriloquism.

Then Dundeed moved. His whole bulk left the leather chair in a disarming pantomime of weightlessness, though the floorboards trembled under my feet in a wave action as dizzying as the deck of a gale-tossed vessel.

And then he was gone. Vanished behind a billowing red velvet curtain: an elegant counterpart to the tattered shadows behind which Cinna's grief remained veiled, save for the sobbing and the throat rasping that was now audibly her own voice scratching at the bars of her mouth.

Behind Dundeed's curtain the only sounds were the shrill ululations that might have been mistaken for the exercised vocalizings of the actor about to step out of his dressing room. Sounds of the masturbator's doll that no ventriloquism can ever bring convincingly to life. So how could we imagine fatherhood to be a role for which he would be suited?

If we would take Dundeed's own belief in a woman's love for the palpable fact, our minds would prove as flaccid as the thin skin he implored Cinna's voice to inflate: like the most popable balloon of childish fancy.

Which is what I meant. Such childishness could not be father to the child, or we wouldn't know what we were thinking of to think it so.

If we can take this proof of Dundeed's infertile longing to be the loose thread of his already loosely woven tale—that he sired an offspring upon Cinna's fair body—can we not be tempted to pull on that thread now? Let the unraveling of that shopworn garb reveal the nakedness of his lying self.

Let the pinching fingers by which we grasp the thread leave a purplish mark on the sagging skin as well, and I'll be well satisfied.

Easy to cast doubt upon an old man's body.

But try to see it from her angle of reflection. What I mean is, venerated maturity is not infrequently a serviceable mirror for aspiring youth. And my young friend here knows, as well as any bright epigone, the temptation to step into the glass where one has caught the fairest image of oneself, however illusory, however chill the immersion in an unknown depth.

Cinna called it her *Theory of Old Men*. And by declaring it so didactically, she attempted to conceal the personal flattery she nevertheless intended to bestow upon me. We sat quite professionally across from one another at the desk in the Sanctuarium Scholasticus. Our first meeting as employer and employee. Need I add mentor and disciple?

I am reminded of this scene, should you wonder, by the stiffness of your own physical presentation to this room, here and now. I remember it by the steeliness of your fervent eye and the forward pitch of your shoulders in the inquisitor's chair. By applying the pressure of my fingertips to the wooden arms of my own chair, here and now, I am bringing out the firmness of the mental focus she inspired then, by what I can only call the zealousness of her voice. The bones in her face radiated her passion as if the brain could sweat its thoughts through the skull with the conviction of a physical exertion.

I can see it. I can hear it. Because I can feel it, here and now.

She declared: "A woman is not only seduced by what scintillates the surface of her skin, as if she were simply a body of water in which the world can see itself reflected. The young man is often smitten by this idea and flexes himself before her."

Her words were laid before me like the most meticulously cleansed findings from the field. I might have beamed to see them arrayed on the desk: a brittle row of tiny teeth, a mandibular fragment, a bone of the inner ear shaped as a minute question mark.

"The older man is his own place," Cinna picked up her account.

"He stands up through the sedimentation of every event of his life, stiffened with excitement by the weight accumulating around him, like an expectant child waiting in a damp swimsuit, to be buried to the neck in sand. But the grains of time weigh with a different valence for him whose temples wear the silvery burnish of his maturity.

"The body filled with its own time and place of experience accumulates the grains of sand within, like the hourglass it feels itself to be.

"The older man feels the brittle transparency of the hand that holds the half filled pint glass. He savors the slaking memory of the things this very hand held before. And because he can see through the reddening fingers that curl around the bottom of the glass, the sloping curve of a breast that once heaved against his heart's grip, in the same hand, in years when nothing reddened but his cheeks, he feels the density of one thing contained within another, strengthening its own gravitational field, like any ball rolling downhill. When throwing his hip to avoid a door handle—it is in the way of his entering a darkened room—he catches the grip of a gaily illuminated dancehall, that whirled blurrily on the same axis of the same body, thirty years before. Thus does the older man assert the indomitability of what those, whose eyes are too densely pigmented with the here and now, would surely lament as lost.

"For he feels the arms of the girl who held his rhythmic self so long before. He feels her touch most urgently under the bruise of the metal flange—that otherwise only opens the door to a darkened room—and he is illuminated by the shape of it.

"You must think of his physique as a photo emulsion. On it the multiple exposures of his flesh to the turbulent world signify the weight that light belies when it strikes our mere consciousness of what we are doing at any given moment. Or better yet, as I've already suggested, think of the weight as a sedimentation, compressed by the hasty footprint of time, and you will begin to appreciate the archeological conceit which I should not have to excavate for you of all people."

She said this last thing with the tip of her tongue prying at the dry corner of her mouth. I should say, since I know how you wonder, that the dryness of your lips, from whence I can see the early dew of your incredulity has begun to evaporate, tell me what I remember.

Then, again, she said, "The density of one thing contained within another strengthens its own gravitational field at the core of the older man's being.

"And it doesn't matter how old the man grows to be. The arms that flex to raise the body trembling from the toilet are stiffened by chords that flexed to raise a hammer over a heartless stone, in the vigor of youthful labors. The stooping of the torso to recover the walking stick carved from an elephant's tusk is levered by the bending of the same torso toward the perfumed bed, and the ivory glimmer of the once kissed brow. The sore feet that shuffle to raise a cloud of dust behind the guiding pace of an encouraging nurse contain the bouncing stride of the athlete's shadow across the finish line. It is all one. The hand holding the parent is the hand holding the hand of the lover, is the hand holding the hand of the beloved child in a solitary grip.

"It is the grip of the older man. And wouldn't any woman be happy to be so held? Does not the blade of grass swept up in the whirlwind know its true weight most momentously against the pull of what it could never resist? Does not the least star in the universe shine more brightly in the centripetal force field of its larger neighbor?

"So my attraction to the older man is, as you might say, natural. I am drawn in by the immensity of what is impacted within the most sagging walls of a body which has sifted time through its narrowly pinched grasp of physical existence. I am drawn into the orbit of the heavier body. But in surrendering to that pull, I am gaining the density of my own weightful presence as a thing of this world that does not merely fall through empty space."

Then I might ask you, can you deny Cinna her "weightful presence" especially as that density now bears upon all our shoulders as nothing less than a dead weight? Pallbearers are we not? Literally. And though you may imagine that I risk self-incrimination to say so, let me point out that I have been saying all along how the weight she bore to me was anything but dead.

By the same token, how do you shrug your shoulders under the burden of swift justice that is still so heavily owed to her murdered body? Is it not heavy?

I might ask you then, if Cinna's *Theory of Old Men* is correct, that the translucence of the body in which everything that has been done in a life is still doing what the muscle and the bone cling to in each new physical effort, then isn't my own assertion correct: that the present remembers the past in every new shiver of sensation that carries us forward, like the breeze upon our face? We carry it, the way it carries the butterfly's wing. Everything past is present in the vital touch.

Is this not what I have been telling you, and why you should believe that I have been telling the truth? Everything past is present in the vital touch.

Take my hand on it.

× × × × ×

If you want to think of what an old man is capable of, consider this.

I had spied his silver-chassis sedan chair, its chariot-sized wheels turned gleamingly in the direction of the footpath. The graded cinder path, shored up with peat-brick shoulders to carry the beam of the wheel chair, led like a tipsy tightrope walker through treacherous mire to the new excavation site. Mound 4.

On the ground adjacent to the cinder path a man would not need a shovel to find his depth. As you know, a man's weight can be his worst enemy, if it's air he wants to breathe.

The lateness of the day was already glooming with rolling clouds of fog. They hung in the misting air like speech blurted in a freezer box.

Was that what attuned me to the faintness of a song warbling within the cottony recesses of the afternoon light? I had no choice but to follow the path. Nor could the footprints I dogged then have been more unambiguous for their extra depth. They were already beginning to fill with black water. An oily rainbow beginning to scum the surface is the telltale of time, is it not?

I am not without my own powers of detection, as I have been trying to persuade you all along. But you don't follow, do you?

The audibility of the song plumped at my approach like a particularly succulent morsel in the mouth. Irresistibly chewable. An aria no less. But words in a language that had no vocabulary, or if it did, would have been undistinguishable from the sound of chewing. The voice was chewing the air, now so thickened with the descending fog that I suddenly realized it was possible for me to stand closer to my prey than would otherwise have been imaginable.

Dundeed's unmistakable shape hulked not four meters from where I froze my foot in midair, not to sound the betraying squish of wet ground, which, truth be told, would have been inaudible under the mashing notes of his song.

I did not yet enjoy what only seconds later I realized was the near invisibility of my own body, heavy as it felt with the cloak of dampness on my shoulder thickening still. Only in the back of my mind did this realization stir doubts about how either of us would find our way back from this outpost in the mire without stumbling into our own unintended burial sites.

No. I was lost in the concentration of Dundeed's hands busily unweaving a long thread of twine from the unwieldy packet that I knew he could not lay upon the ground without risking his balance.

You've seen how quickly the stone sinks in our mire. Who can resist hurling the heaviest stone within reach, just to see it disappear?

And yet you must ask, how could a man who should not have been able to raise himself from his seat have been able to heft the burlap-wrapped packet, not to mention the shovel that he had also lumbered this distance from his wheelchair, without the help of another hand?

Standing on the mounded atoll—the dampness clouding sight and soon to set my vigilant eye adrift from my precarious foot—I asked myself how could he be laboring upon a hole that was already deep enough to hide his knees? How could he be laboring with such gusto that it called a song to his lips and lifted his voice well above my head?

For all the mystery of that moment I can tell you, close as I stood to the industrious noise of him then, there was nothing mysterious about what he made ready to lower into the hole. Only three legs visible. But it was unmistakably the grizzled muzzle of a small dog, peering lifelessly—of this there was no doubt—from under the lofting flap of its burlap wrapper.

Deep as Dundeed was in the hole at this point, it would have been easy for him simply to reach out and—for whatever unfathomable reason was already inscrutably working at this depth—draw the thing directly into his chest.

I expected it, like a person whose mind is beaded in attention to the next resounding note from a dripping faucet.

But instead of letting his arms become buoyant with the next chorus of the still booming song, instead of reaching out at breast level to swell his song with the weight of the dog's body against his chest, he stooped deeper. He absconded from the nets of my surveilling gaze.

The song hung in the air above the hole like his own ghostliness. The rapidly condensing breeze lent an ectoplasmic lurch to the fading palpability of the sound.

And then perfect silence.

Above ground, I could see the burlap covering borne back by the same breeze-stroke to reveal the full body of the dog. I could see that what I had naturally taken for the fur, albeit mortified like ringlets of cold tar, was neither animal nor mineral altogether. Because it was the dead earth itself that possessed the clearly mummified shape of that mammalian being. The muscular flesh had been osmotically replaced by the mineral content of dead grass and reeds. The body is thus made buoyant by decay. Only the white of the cranial occiput showed—through the dun color of the peated physique—the evidence of the skeleton within, like a lurking eye. Buried inside itself. And then of course I realized. Light as an egg carton, it would have been, to be carried all that distance under the arm of a man with a shovel in the other hand.

What first reappeared from the faintly respiring rim of the hole was not the scintillating blade of the shovel, but the very same arms I had earlier expected would dispatch the specimen lying above ground into its freshly dug depths. Now they arose, brimming with remains of the very same dog.

Or so it seemed. But there were two dogs now laid side by side at the edge of the cut. And Dundeed himself remained shoulder deep in the trench. Did I wonder, with some impish tickle of malice, that he had inadvertently dug his own grave? So intent on his mysterious digging, perhaps he had forgotten the perfectly obvious height and weight of his own burdensome physique, which no strength of his fatted arms could ever render buoyant enough to float easefully to the surface?

Did I ponder this with a shocked grimace at my own capacity for malicious surmise?

I did not. Because, to my greater shock, the extended arms merely reached for the waiting burden of the first dog and lowered it in place of the likeness he had just removed. More than my wonder at the feats of physical labor, that so fleetly outstripped the sweating corpulence of his physical presence, was my trembling awareness of what it must mean.

Forgery. What I had never even conceived could be contemplated was too apparent to be denied. And a likeness of dogs was the least of my defamatory deductions.

An archeologist burying a bone is a dog to his profession. What he puts into the ground, should he so misstep the path of his professional code, is his own time, an unwanted footprint that confuses the trail leading back into the historical dusk lands. He doesn't want to put anything *into* the ground. He is an excavator, not an inseminator. The fact that the inventory of Dundeed's most celebrated specimens already had such a thespian cast to them was merely a corroborating element of my conviction that, in this case, both were confabulated dogs. They might as well have been the mythic guardians of some sulphurous portal to hell, as bona fide specimens for the laboratory, where the carboniferous cell is made to unmask itself under the inveigling meniscus of the microscope.

What did I know, I had to ask. I felt summoned to *your* detective duty by my most dutiful sense of the science (indeed it is a science) I serve.

I hope you understand that Dundeed is not the only sleuth of resemblances here.

But the similarity I observed then would be more comprehensible to you perhaps by analogy with the painter. I mean the forgery artist. His brushstroke is more than a doubling of what is real. Or should I say, really artful? The bristles come together like a tongue dipped in the taste of such familiarity that one has no desire to eat.

I knew it then. One dog replaced another, not as the false thing is put in the place of the true, but as the more refined falsity seduces one's deceit to a truer attempt. I know I'm making sense.

Think of it. What has Dundeed always been but the better image of a scientist? And what of the *finds* that lavished such praise upon him? Were they not the fawning hounds of fame themselves, lapping at the master's salted palm?

Here on the open heath: two dogs instead of one dog. Identical. The fact that there are two tells you that one of them is *preferable*. The specter of Dundeed, shoulder deep in the freshly cut trench and still puffing with the effort of his laborious transaction—for I swear the mists miraculously cleared with the onset of my detective lucidity—tells you that one of the dogs is better than the other. In someone's mind.

Whom would you think?

Only the pride of the forger, more naked and lascivious—or else would we marvel at it?—than that of the artist himself, would inspire such rabid perfectionism.

But can it be done, you marvel? In this case, is it not all too perishable flesh that must be copied? Can nature be tampered with as frivolously as pigment? Doesn't the animal roundedness or vegetable process of its reality defy the falsifier's art?

Let me tell you. The cell has an inside and an out. Its permeability is the secret of mummification, though my colleagues quibble over the aptness of a term that contaminates knowledge of natural process with a human artifice that only specialists have knowledge of. We are no Egyptians here. We are not priests and priestesses of the sacred asp. To the contrary. Our science belongs to nature, like a birthmark. That explains why it would be so easy to disfigure a natural truth with a dissembling nature.

Water is all you need: a mordant acidity in the mix, a pressurized medium, to exert the semblance of time's impress. Nothing more is needed to conjure a date in antiquity and imprint it on the physical specimen. The flesh will succor the air of credulity that breathes its droughty odour.

What I mean to say is: one of the dogs is better than the other.

Do you not comprehend it yet? One of the dogs is a better specimen than the other. That is what has harried the criminal back to the scene of the crime. To purify the lie of its technical crudities. Only the body-forger himself knows there may be a hair that could be dried to a more perfect roughness. A tooth could be better tarnished with vinegar pus. A fold in the brown underbelly could be made to better mime the intestinal undulation of the gases in their final passage. And there are items that could be lodged between the toe-pads of the desiccated paw, undisguised evidence of the path the animal trod, on its four legs. A bead of amber gilding a perfect flea. A clod of human shite crumbly as a cookie. A shard of egg shell cragged as a tooth. Dundeed must have thought better of the second specimen. Pride of workmanship is proportionate to the sincerity of deceit.

Am I solving it for you? The man you would take to be too fat for feats of physical agility—too withered with age under the disguise of that corpulence—turns out to be the most dedicated falsifier of the flesh. And remarkably robust in his capacity as a craftsman of forfeiture, whose intent is cellular, whose dexterity has microscopic implications.

Now think of the expanse of Dundeed's career and consider the mandate for closer inspection of his achievement.

More than one hundred specimens are illuminated in the crystal display cases of Mr. Doyle's museum. Posed like so many puppets on the stage of a children's entertainment? You have to consider the possibility, do you not?

And when you do, consider also the bent fingers of the puppeteer. Think of the knots they have tied.

The public enthusiasm, inveigled by the theater of Dundeed's discoveries, festoons his reputation as a man of scientific accomplishment. But, because every new "find" proved a more imaginative incitement for the audience's desire to visit the past—each new specimen a more storied phenomenon—I realize, we should have proved more skeptical of the unrehearsed artifice of such scientific endeavor. How like a repertory is the inventory of Dundee's collection. How like a darkened auditorium was the drama of his discoveries. We might have thought worse of the popularity we ourselves enjoyed in the footlights of Dundeed's impressarioism.

If that is so, we must think worse now.

Think that the deceiver who fleshes the stern bone of fact with lascivious fiction is also the artificer. His skills, when we recognize them, enable us to see through the fiction of his physical enfeeblement to the capable fact of a murderous nature.

x x x x x

FIELD INVENTORY: (November 3, 1979) Specimen #3, Crate #39

Horse. Extraction unknown. Hide reddened with umber grease and berry paste. Measuring 2 meters, 46 centimeters from bite to tail. The abdominal cavity cleansed of organs and fitted for the enclosure of a small human.

Male: 1 meter, 68 centimeters sutured within the cavity by a coarse hempen thread. The thread is knotted around short briar sticks, sharpened at their ends and longitudinally woven into the hide at both extremities of the suture.

Age of the human male approximated between 17 and 19. The body is so closely adapted to the shape of the cavity as to belie its own skeletal structure. The skin is colored with the dun of the cavity it fills. Only one distinguishing mark: the tongue, easily visible through the pouted lips, is pierced with a tiny beak. Perhaps a hummingbird.

Owing to an unannotated circumstance of the excavation, all the skeletal ligatures of the horse's physique are broken, as if by an effort to draw it from its interment with dragging hands.

x x x x x

But I have my book...

My book will say...

The find for which I am best known is the museum's treasure.

An incarnadine horse! But the horse's secret was my real discovery: a man inside it like its own foal. And so a ritual unimaginable before the letter of scientific fact declared its being so.

This is what I remember. I could immediately appreciate the importance of the specimen. Its distinction was fully proportionate to the length of the story it told. Compared with the aura of unstoried time so mutely adorning the severed heads and limbs, the bodies trussed and bagged that made up the greater portion of our inventory, the horse and its unconventional rider bespoke themselves of an event.

And who but the scientist knows better the duty to present such a discovery, fully faithful to the corpuscle of its moment in living time? Who but the scientist knows best the responsibility to say that something happened?

The ringing marble rotunda that divided the two halves of our museum wing like the midday chime had always been reserved for such a centerpiece.

I had my trusted artisans around me for the exalting work of doing justice to that space.

The horse and rider lay in their discrete spaces, uncrated and carefully prepared for handling. To the unknowledgeable eye their desiccated forms might have been mistaken for bedraggled costuming, discarded on the marble dance floor of a party that had lasted well beyond the announced hour of its festivity. Appearing nearly two dimensional in their state of cellular compression, the challenge of these specimens stood out from their crumpled demeanor: to flex this slack clothing with the bodyful vigor of an account—whatever account we might give—of the ritual that had been so primally their occasion.

Exhibition. To exhibit. The word means more than to make visible: to submit for credulity's sake. Our charge was just that: to make what was quite unarguably and unalterably visible, believable.

Mr. Levant Doyle—amateur archeologist, friend of the National Society, patron of the museum—himself stood by. Hadn't his astrological charts determined the day our work was meant to begin? A patron in every way.

And yet the tapping of his silver-tipped walking stick—the silver on the other end was fashioned into a medusa head, even more tentacled by the fingers of his impatient grip—kept a separate time. A time distinct from the clocks and calendars that Doyle believed required constant, anxious surveillance in relation to the motions of the moon and stars, if one were to escape a malign fate. The tapping of his stick, which was the metronome of our working relationship, told another story.

Astrologist first, but banker and amateur archeologist he was no less.

And if the burnished obsidian and gold Pisces medallion ring he wore upon his left hand was the talisman of the vocation of astrology, the black bowler hat with the sealskin sheen and the khaki jodhpur pants, which he sported beneath the banker's striped waistcoat, were sacred to the other selves that made him, as he often said, so mosaically himself.

But he knew better than to speak as I ordered the scaffolding to be wheeled into place beneath the sepulchral dome of the exhibition space.

My blueprint ordained a steel armature be erected, its absolute rigidity disguised by a titanium suspension system. Virtually invisible filaments of the lightest metallic fiber on earth would allow the slightest vibration to be conducted—by a tiny electric motor—to the steel skeletons from which the specimens would be hung, apparently loosely in the billowing crystalline air of the columnar display case. But, as if the whole thing were a tiny glass-domed hand toy, which when upended with a spasmodic motion of the wrist produced a quaint scene of snowfall, there would descend through the sealed chamber of glass—a trick of double pane construction—an unceasing curtain of earthen particles, brown and black clods, like a cloud of insects frenzied by a transparent pane.

The illusion of passage through a medium. Bog water and sucking sediment. This was what we sought to conjure. A coagulation of elements, foretold to become another world where desiccation would flourish as a preservative of all that was buried within it. Through this deliberate obfuscation of the specimens thus suspended within the case, the museum visitor would have a view of everything that could change into something else and remain somehow the same. And yet the viewer would feel that it was all happening here and now. Would know it.

See the horse, its long-legged stride bereft of any purchase upon solid ground, the whole physique raked forward by the shifting weight of its human cargo. See the horse in the ritual moment of its downward trajectory through the mire, a sinking vessel. But more important, see that we have taken a modest liberty.

What would an exhibit be if the thing to be rendered visible kept a secret from the viewer? Only seeing is believing, is it not? Isn't that what we say?

So see that we have found a way to reveal the hidden human presence in the horse's otherwise unfathomable draught, without resorting to the pedantic theatrics of cross section or vivisectional splayen.

We have opened a dozen stitches in the otherwise faithfully re-sutured seam of the abdominal cavity. We have dangled an arm. We have seen the mistake of dangling it too far toward the posterior of the animal's anatomy. It is the authentic arm, still crooked in a desperately interrogative angle against the wall of its confinement, but now turned so that the hand, which was found flattened against an unyielding surface, unfurls from the animal's girth in a gesture, almost of salutation, into the artfully confected ambience of bog water and accumulating sediment. Escape? Inescapable doom?

Let the viewer decide for herself.

We wished only to draw the curtain of time from the form of the ritual. Its meaning escapes us in any case. Let the curtain stay down if it merely teases idle speculation. Science is bound to remain disinterested where mere speculation is all that solicits our belief.

But I have almost forgotten—and isn't that why I am bound

to write it all down in my book in the first place?—my only serious brush with the quibble of artistic license, my only serious quarrel with Mr. Doyle's otherwise impeccable patronage.

Even my reader may have forgotten the human remainder.

What were we to do with the residual specimen of a one-armed man whose missing limb already served so eloquently to conjure the invisible presence weighing so oppressively upon us now? We contemplated our choices: sequestering it in a numbered crib in the museum's dark crypt, or exhibiting it one-armed in some necessarily peripheral and shadowy corner of the museum. But I knew that however far removed it might be from the rotunda, the hawkish eye of an unexpectedly astute museum visitor, moving in some increasingly focused transit from that peripheral point of curiosity to the centerpiece of our exhibition hall, would easily infer that the missing torso was found! And then we would be assailed with the charge of tampering with the historical fact.

Then would not the modest contrivance of our attempt to show something to eyes that would not otherwise see, become itself, and confoundingly enough, the most infamous exhibition of the entire museum? I told Mr. Doyle—who was adamantly opposed to hiding a valued specimen, even in the most airtight vault of safe keeping, let alone within the draft of a horse—that it would be equally unacceptable to permit our concerted efforts to show it all, become themselves a spectacle of self-mockery, a pretext for fingers to point, a licensing of the word "fraud" upon the lips—already wet with jealousy—of our professional foes. All the easier for them to spit upon our achievements within these walls.

Mr. Doyle lifted his steel-rimmed spectacles from the red-grooved bridge of his nose. The gleam of the Pisces insignia adorning his ring finger glittered like the toss of a coin. His weight upon the walking stick silenced the nervous tapping that was ordinarily the code of our rapport.

"Let me share a vision with you," he offered.

"Let's imagine what the squinty-eyed visitor would want to see, if he were to be led by his own stammering imagination, to follow the thoughts of the man inside. Inside the horse.

"And haven't you grimaced yourself at our waste of the most mysterious fact of the case: the tongue pierced by a beak? 'A mastery *wrapped in an enigma,' didn't you say it yourself? Witty, yes. But how does one exhibit the mystery of a Chinese box without opening the box and spoiling the mystery?*

"Here is what I propose. Let us take the head. Only the head! Let us put it aloft in the display case. More titanium wires if you like. Let it sway. Let us think of it as winged with the last thoughts of that body struggling to be free of the equine girth. Let us enhance the effect by secreting within the head itself—which is already secretive beyond our poor powers of artifice—a loudspeaker no bigger than a sparrow's throat.

"Let us imagine the music of birds thus emanating from the recesses of that head and so at a convincing height above the barely swimming eyes of the agog spectator. The spectator is already succumbing to the effect like the swimmer who has given up the shore, who longs for gills and burning mouthfuls of water. He is hearing the chirp of the victim's most frightful thoughts carried on the wing of the most desperate hope. He is already living behind the glass.

"Need I explain the beauty that shines through this? Can a curator who so nakedly exhibits the artifice of the display case be accused of any unlicensed artfulness? Cannot science, in that way, be licensed by art?"

The tight-lipped smile that tore at the corners of Doyle's mouth, made of the flat colorless cheeks and unlined forehead a brittle paper mask. My hand trembled with all the resistance I could muster against an impulse to seize the briar stick from Doyle's smug grip and poke through the mask. The steel tip, fashioned into a talon of the medusa's monstrosity, would have made its jagged point.

Instead I let my bottom jaw swing loose. Relaxed my tongue against the lower row of teeth where the most vehement speech gains its momentum and merely exhaled the tempestuous breath that wanted trees to blow down in its path.

"Mr. Doyle," I let the words melt over the controlled flame of my patient explanation, "Science is solicitous of nothing but fact. Yes, as I've said many times, you are too much the aesthete. But what is pleasing is seldom what is true.

"Mr. Taste is your man for these indulgences. He has a penchant for likenesses, like you. And for the self-justifying fetish they cultivate. As I assured you on so many such occasions, in science there is nothing to justify."

And I turned back to the cluttered surface of the walnut escritoire, attempted a cooling immersion in the blue-printed plans that eddied around me.

Then: "But the beauty. The beauty is that we call attention to the fact of our tampering with the specimen! So there is nothing of unreality to be found in it. They will only know that our feeling for the thing is of the first order of sincerity. And the more we tamper, the truer it must become by that standard."

He had not shut his mouth, the key to which I believed I had deftly palmed by the logic of my final declaration to him. Had a bird flown out of his mouth I couldn't have been more startled. Nor more outraged.

The silver-tipped cane flew further than the bird. The blood in his mouth surged more improbably. But I remain at a loss to comprehend how it happened at all. Or that it all happened.

My hands hung, open-palmed at my sides, white doves of passivity. I was standing. I had been seated behind the overturned escritoire. The splashes of blue-print that puddled at my feet ran into the sprawl of Mr. Doyle's outstretched arms and legs. How flat he made the floor appear.

I marveled that the magnifying glass, which I used to guide my eye into the most intricate spaces of the elaborately filigreed blue-prints, still swung by its leather thong from my neck. But its thick bubble of convexity had burst from the gunmetal frame.

The room around us, the Sanctuarium Scholasticus, *was otherwise undisturbed, and silent as the tomb it was meant to be.*

"My dear sir," I extended a hand to Doyle's dishevelment.

His acceptance of it was only more puzzling for my discovery of the magnifying lens in his grip, now silently returned to me. It lay along the bulging lifeline of the hand by which I raised him—the other arm dangling behind—to his unsteady legs.

After a fit of almost inaudible sniffling and a humid cough, Mr. Doyle recomposed his face, passing a hand over the eyes, replacing the steel-rimmed spectacles, mopping the corners of the mouth with the handkerchief that I had mistaken for a crisp insignia illusionistically embroidered above the breast pocket of the banker's waistcoat.

"You'll forgive me I'm sure," he smiled a dimpled apology, out of what knowledge of the situation that merited such groveling formality I cannot begin to wonder.

But it had the effect of dignifying my dismay. I calmly turned the upended escritoire back onto its squat legs. I patted my own clothes, tucked the flaps of my breast pockets back into their places. I cleared my throat. I licked my lips before I spoke again.

"Well then, we must be finished here. Let's have a drink, shall we?"

How easy it is to remember while I am writing it all down. Even though I know I am writing the epitaph of my coming forgetfulness, I am solaced by the thought of re-reading it from the other side. With this pen I am signing a good faith contract with that other one, the reader who is as unknown to me as I am to him, though we shall soon be the same person.

I am content to pass on this legacy, though I know it may be misunderstood. For, whatever unjust interpretations may cloud the scene I have exhibited in these pages, it remains an event. The event is fixed forever by the bright lines of my description. They block the action definitively, whatever clouds of doubt may momentarily darken the stage. Like all mercurial weather, the clouds will pass.

When I told you that Cinna was like my mother, I still insist I did not digress or distort the flow of events as you wished me to recount them then. I said she loved me for my childlike innocence. Is it not my innocence that you implore me to speak of still?

I may even be innocent of the appearance of obfuscation, if what I recall of my childhood now can shed some light on the mystery that remains yours to solve. Do you not agree?

My father was not a heavy man like this one here, so let's not lumber toward unduly predictable conclusions. My father was a stiff reed of a man, all the better suited to dispense the punishments that he might have believed were his calling into this world.

If my mother had been placed on this earth to furnish her son's understanding of love, my father's role was to test her capacity for it.

A sheep man, he called himself when suffering social introductions. I never thought it required explanation. For me his voice was always tensed with the zither sibilance of the reed he beat the air with to drive the sheep in and out of the chicken wire pens. Though of course he never drove the herds himself. He was the landlord after all. Made rich, not by sheep, but by chickens, of which he never spoke.

And I should clarify at the outset, that the meaning of innocence for me has nothing to do with the unblemished wool of the baby lamb, though I know the feel of it as well as the itch of my own scalp. I learned the meaning of innocence—my own never less pristine than the lamby nap—from the wolfish shadow of my father's rage.

The shadow of the wolf had lunged across my mother's path long before I was born. The body of the wolf hobbled my own path when he leapt to take my mother's place. He was her abductor from the start. He weaned her from me before I had ever tasted the full breast. At his command, she disappeared to other rooms of the house, other worlds as far as I knew. For the first three years of my life her presence was as wavering as a face in water. Other faces shone more durably over my cradle—and later over the shadowy footboard of my boy's bed—during the recurring seasons of her absence. Aunts, uncles, upstairs maids, unoccupied shepherds lowly sounding their pan-pipes, strangers with sorrowfully bowed heads. Often tearful. Often burbling the dirge music of a lullaby. Often pouting. Often blowing kisses that bubbled with salty grief.

Though my father seemed to be present to me only within earshot of my mother's sobbing—a ghostliness audible from a connecting hallway—he was ever her eclipse. He was fiery against the velveteen blackness of her absence: his face florid with the blood of his latest outburst, as if smeared with the costume rouge for a clownish antic, the arms and legs stricken in the pose of a dizzy tightrope walker, the dishevelment of his clothing dampened by the close escape from the lion's quick paw. He stood before me in a veritable circus state of emotional agitation. I am told my laughter coagulated his hands into white fists.

But when my mother returned from her forced exiles—on her intermittent returns—I saw the blue shadows of those fists cast upon her cheeks. I saw her eyelids, like curtains hanging off their hooks, hooding the blood-flecked whites of her eyes. I understood the stooped posture by which she clenched the knuckles of pain so deeply socketed in her gut.

For a man who had wanted no children—weren't these the words that hammered his blows home from a distant room, wasn't this his grievance against my mother for which no punishment would ever suffice?—he was always fascinated to examine the look of privation this knowledge visited on my upturned face. Wordlessly, he enquired into the mystery of my empty eyes. And yet, ruminating as he was in his scrutiny of my tiny person, he never proposed a single question. Was it because he knew the answer already? Or was it because he was embarrassed not to know?

Considering his aversion to the thought, let alone the inhaling and exhaling bodily presence of children, my father should have ignored me. But he watched incessantly. As absent as he rendered my mother, he made himself that much more intently present to the impact of that abandonment upon the bewildered child, and with a diligence that could easily have been mistaken for fatherly devotion. He observed my loneliness as closely as the researcher eyes the bubble rising slowly, slowly in the experimental test tube. There was, after all, nothing between us but time, the limpid medium in which I grew.

I remember only one event that tinctured the medium of time with some communication between us.

Sunlight washed the floorboards of the summerhouse porch with a slippery sheen. I knew it by my reflection, swimming up to me on all fours. A crawling tiddler laps to his reflection like a wobbly-footed puppy laps to a saucer of milk. The voices that trembled on the taut surface of that reflection wore heavy shoes. Clattering toward the porch steps. One pair like falling rocks. The other like water quickening in its passage over the rocks. Did I know what I heard before it twitched my ears?

Holding her by the neck my father drove my mother in front of him, walking her backwards towards the invisible steps. My father's forearms seemed positively furred with their fury. My mother's naked white arms hung as loosely behind her as if she were a doll in the grip of something that could lift her entirely off the ground to hurl her further.

But my father was not relinquishing his grip. He was caught with her in such a complicated dance step of rage that, like an entanglement of rope, or the uncoiled garden hose at their feet, it threatened to put them both off balance.

Others heard the suspenseful music of that mounting struggle: a perspiring gardener spilling hose-water on his shoes, a kerchiefed aunt in sunglasses catching up the golden hem of her sundress in red hands, a nurse bearing a clinking tray of freshly washed bottles. As violent as the frenzy of my parents' altercation was, the approaching bodies of these witnesses were seized by inversely proportionate states of sudden arrest. Stupefied by the spectacle. Speechless. As caught in the shocking lucidity of the all-revealing sunlight, as butterflies pinned under a pane of glass.

Did my father raise his fist against that glass when he spied me so dazzling sprawled at his feet and so precipitously in danger of being swept into the vortex of their fury?

One finger extruded from the fist as it swung in my direction. Accusation? Admonition? Unimaginable gesture of parental regard?

Who will ever know? The distracted hand released my mother's throat into the air. It flew. Having pirouetted in the direction of some plausible blue escape, she had stepped blindly into empty air. The steep flight of porch steps clipped her wings.

As if imploring the sky for support she fell with her hands in the air, and so upon the points of her elbows. Powdered bones. And yet they broke her fall, saved her face and her knees from those disfigurements that cast a permanent shadow over the pained body.

My father's arms were a curious refuge for the brief moments in which he struggled to know where to set me down. I never saw my mother fall.

Am I remembering correctly? You say you have to ask? I have confused you so?

Ask him—the weight of time himself—who sits so saggingly beside you. Ask him if he remembers any discrepancy in my account. You must challenge him to list the variances between what I say now and what I said then. Then you will be aptly reminded of the difference between us.

Have I made my point?

He takes me for his father, if I'm not mistaken. Or is his oh-so-vibrant projection of me as the sadistic parent merely the feeble masquerade of the guilty conscience that shrinks inside him like the harmed child he persists in being?

Yes. Let's resist the temptation to dabble in the bog waters of the unconscious, shall we? Trust me. Nothing is preserved there except the softest tissues of the brain, which continuously ooze the most fanciful filth of the warped imagination.

I will tell you instead what we have witnessed together, Roscoe Taste and I, as curators of the peat. You have to admit it is fertile ground for suffering thoughts of the worst that could be done by one man to another.

But we have been partners too. We have shared a find site. We have shared the glory.

How would I remember, you think to ask?

Memory is a mystery, as is everything else in life, I'm sure a detective would have to agree. Sometimes, rarely, my memory revisits me. An unexpected guest, to be sure. There is not even a knocking at the door, only a sudden presence, intimate and familiar. And who is at home, you might snidely inquire, to be so visited? It is I, who here and now accepts whatever comes as more of myself. You know from looking at me that I am a man of insatiable appetite. So why should you demur my telling you what I know in this moment of spontaneous lucidity, which I unhesitatingly imbibe as the elixir of life. Imbibe with me. Listen. Be attentive. Have faith in what comes naturally. Drink. Drink my health, that in this fragile but crystalline decanter of fleeting time, a memory, a real memory, is brimming.

By appointment of the university, I was Roscoe Taste's first team leader. He was sent to me. He was attached to my operation. But he was the finder. I give him credit. I have never taken anything from him that was his to own.

We pitched our tent together on what we assured ourselves was the periphery of the new excavation site. The four corners of the quadrant flew the flags of the university's insignia—he wore it upon the breast pocket of his woolen jacket, a gold phoenix splayed upon a murex field. The fluttering of the flags sounded the anthem of a new phase of the exploration of Blackman's Heath.

His deference to me in those days was breathtaking. He 'sirred' me obsequiously. He prepared my meals. He even carried my shovel. Our tent was his butler's pantry. Everything was organized to finesse his service to me. Every comfort deferred to my preference. He was honored to offer me the solitary cot, the privilege to sleep above ground, while he contented himself to lie in a harshly camphorated sleeping bag, laid directly onto the heath.

And that was *his* good fortune.

As he slept, the discomfort of the ground beneath him wriggling in his vertebrae, wormed its way into his dream, so that he awoke with a visionary fervor. He wanted to dig out the patch of ground on which he had so fruitlessly attempted sleep. By the time I kneaded the sleep from my eyes, he had already swept away the flimsy covering of the sleeping bag, had already ignited the oil lamp, setting his shadow atremble beneath its hissing flame, was already letting his fingers spread themselves telepathically over the sphagnum crust, feeling for the pulse of the dream.

He barely needed a brush to find the purpose of his efforts. Two strokes of the wrist revealed the remains of a human backbone. Almost entirely skeletal but varnished with a thin epidermis, shriveled to the bone like the most vehemently indrawn breath.

The exposure to air would have precipitated this decay. But perhaps the head and the other extremities, more deeply embedded in the turf would yet be plumped with the soft tissue of their human semblances. For the body was turned in the attitude of a drowning victim, head and limbs dangling from the trunk as through a liquid depth. The spine, risen like a dorsal fin, or the keel of an unfortunate boat, arched into view with a buoyancy that floated high expectations among the members of the team. They quickly gathered around the light.

And yes, by dint of our digging, as the earth ebbed to the contours of a proper trench around the emerging physique, the flesh began to flow back to the bone. Or so it seemed. The inverse proportion of air to earth that had occasioned this specimen's mummification registered, in mirror reflection, as a subtle displacement of the biceps to the forearms, the toned muscle of the forearms to the fingers of the hands that gestured like rubber gloves squeezed full with water. Likewise the natural swell of the thighs seemed to have slipped to the calves, the muscle tone of the calves to the feet, plumped to the toes with preservative being.

But the head, dangling on the delicate link-by-link filigree of neck vertebrae was the prize jewel of the specimen.

A lush fall of ochre hair hung from the back of the head like a curtain over the face. My assistant, Roscoe Taste, was again obedient to my instructional hand. After the inspirational moment of impetuous discovery, after the feverish independence of the first brushstrokes that proved his intuition sound, he now manipulated the hand spade to my meticulous specifications, until the entire specimen lay upon its peated bier, an intaglio relief, that seemed to embrace the medium of which it was carved with near lascivious abandon. Left high and dry by the excavation process, the body veritably clutched the pedestal of peat upon which it now seemed to have been raised.

The removal of the head could now be attempted, so we might see what face the passionate body wore upon its ecstatic posture. Man or woman? The length of the hair meant nothing. The saddle sheen of the deflated buttocks, slung upon fairly naked pelvic bones, meant nothing.

Cut with a fine-toothed saw at the third vertebrae, the turf brick in which the face was imprinted, and still so densely matted with hair, could be hefted out of the quarrying trench and turned gingerly upon a linen hammock, stretched for this purpose between two wooden struts at either end of the worktable. The hammock would support the slow and patient labor of etching the face without disfiguring the back of the head, delicate as a bird's nest built of mud. And perhaps because the head swung in the hammock like the peaceful weight of a baby, Roscoe Taste began to hum a lullaby while he worked.

Scimitar tweezers, cotton swabs, vials of cleansing oil, shiny spatulas, and finger trowels were all at his disposal. The industrious rhythm of his hands harmonized effortlessly with the song in his throat. Nature seemed to be taking its course while we waited.

And it was almost the face of a baby when it was revealed, when the last strands of mineral-coarsened hair had been tweezed from the surprisingly high cheekbones and aquiline nose. We could see that the curtain of hair, dawning more brightly orange under the glare of a midday sun—we had been up since well before dawn—had effected a miraculous preservation. It was a face without blemish. Not only was the skin somehow untainted by the dingy passage of nitrogen gases, which is of course the vital respiration of the mummifying process, but it was unwrinkled by any age. Neither its own time nor ours had left the subtlest tidemark. Rather, the skin seemed to have been kissed with the hue of an unripe strawberry, turning more ardently in the direction of the sun. The lips had drunk more deeply of that light and were filled to the point of translucence with it. The high brow fairly crowned the face with an alabaster aura of everlasting youth.

Only the eyes had gone black, but nonetheless shone with the knowledge of atrocity for which this dig site was already becoming notorious in the records of our profession.

Where the experts had thought to unearth a primitive mill, even a granary, temples to common human necessity, yeasty germs of compassionate community, they had uncovered instead the ritual ground of the most vehement punishments.

So, revelation that it was, in its extraordinary state of preservation, the face told us nothing of its nature, beyond the possibility of its termination at the end of a hot, if not flaming, stick. Whatever gouged the eyes charred the sockets. The thick smudge of carbonized wood certainly penetrated to the brain.

Man or woman? How could we tell even that simple fact from a face so neutered? Wouldn't you agree that what we can see depends for its certainty upon what we can see looking back at us? After all, isn't that why there are three of us in this room? Here and now?

Here and now things are as they ever were. Are they not?

In any case, disappointed as we were, we knew the body would show us what we failed to see in the face. The organs of the sex—the penis of the man, the breasts of the woman—because they are the most pendulous, would certainly be the best preserved. The ripest fruits of the process.

One must hew the peat with a reticent hand to bring out the form of what it conceals, because the matter of the medium and the matter of what is preserved within it are osmotically joined under one skin.

And I must say Roscoe Taste's trowel hand is as sensitive as any I have seen in its discernment of the wavering line between one nature and another.

And when the small but pertly pointed breasts of our red tressed beauty were skillfully freed from the coarse bodice of compressed root matter and intricate leaf mesh, we satisfied ourselves that we had rescued an art treasure of femininity. We would have been no less awed by a torso of Venus turned out of the earth at the steps of a ruined temple.

The work could have paused then, with the rest of the body still girdled in its uncarved block of peat. We had not slept. The rays of the sun had lengthened across our backs like the lashes of the slave driver's whip. Our weariness had already been amply rewarded with loveliness sufficient to justify a special exhibit in the newest hall of Mr. Doyle's museum.

But the unjust cause of her punishment was still unrevealed. And so the block of peat in which her hips and thighs still floated upon an opaque surface weighed that much more heavily upon our efforts to continue.

Now I must say we were all misled in our expectations of what else might be revealed here. For that reason, if no other, Roscoe had to be forgiven his hand's misstep. We were all watching. We were all witnesses to the fading light. Nevertheless, we had all urged his consummation of the act.

Therefore: following the line of the groin with deft adherence to the pubic bone concealed within it, and finding, in the smallest bones of his own wrist, a delicate attunement with the receding contour of the pudenda, with the minute incisiveness of the cleft, where the body ends in its own beginning, so you might say, the mirrory knife edge of Roscoe's trowel severed what it was meant to discover.

Our collective gasp guttered the flame of the candle by which Roscoe Taste was required to work in this dimmest ebb of daylight. Like the shadows that fall away when the light goes on in a cluttered room, the lump of formless peat that had fallen away from the knife and broken softly upon Taste's shoe revealed its unimaginable substance, its real gravitational center, against which any body acclimated to the dark would helplessly stumble. The black rays of pain will shine through this body, a blinding glare of sensation.

It was of course the entire genitalia of the opposite sex that Roscoe Taste now stooped to recover and thrust so awkwardly, like a roughly gathered bouquet, into the light of what scrutiny we could muster from our surprise. Taste's gesture across the face of the candle garishly reanimated the shadow world out of which his confusion with the knife edge no doubt arose.

The cowled head of the penis was like a tightly wrapped grape leaf. The shaft looked like nothing so much as the unmolded casting of an earthen tunnel, ivy twined with root tracings, and worm runs. The unnaturally swollen scrotal sack frayed like a cut rope where it had been severed from the body was intact, stubbled like the prominent chin of an adolescent. They cast transmogrifying shadows onto the slack white faces huddled for this inspection around the resuscitated candlelight.

"Freak of nature."

In his voice we heard the metallic tipping of the brass scale by which Roscoe Taste judged this specimen less valuable than the natural beauty he had already imagined to be a more estimable balance against the exquisite effort of his excavation. Beauty would have been the perfect counterweight to his professional dream, the gravity that would have started the noble grandfather clock of archeological history ticking for the record of an illustrious career.

Isn't it like the vanity of the man of taste to be so easily seduced by beauty? How little sympathy for life it shows.

Or must we be more forgiving of a man who is himself still the victimized child, in all the recurring fears that strike like sudden lightning in the forest of his brain? Such are the liabilities of a perfect memory.

Perhaps this explains why Roscoe Taste could not savor the pathos of our discovery. The "beauty" of this specimen's "fit" with the story we were piecing together, like some sinister puzzle spread out on the rough contours of this persecuted ground all around us, was entirely lost on him. No doubt the pattern of his own childhood punishments had inculcated a natural aversion to the motive for violence so nakedly revealed, and however unwittingly—even innocently—compounded by the errant knife edge of his own trowel. So much were his senses discombobulated by the revelations of the moment, that his well-trained eye missed the glaring evidence of the act itself, by which our fair and doubly-sexed youth had been dispatched.

Between the legs. Where else would the viciousness be most meaningful to the narrow-eyed perpetrators of the deed?

What the rest of us had already taken—by what deficit of *our* powers of observation I am ashamed to query—to be follicles of pubescent hair growth, that even the most grievously maimed human scrotum would present to the anatomist's eye, prickled with a more painful knowledge when remanded to the sense of touch.

Wooden pins. It was beyond our imagining how they could have been milled so fine. But each nodular follicle was in truth the point of a pin.

Each pin was sharp at both ends. And small enough to have been swallowed whole within the walls of the tormented organ. There would have been no possibility of withdrawing the pin once inserted. But that of course was the cruel intention.

In other words each pin was small enough to have disappeared into the very sensations that would have pricked all visibility with the wild contortions of the victim's suffering. They would have made the spectacle of the victim, lurching helplessly over the brink of bog waters, a sufficient entertainment for the hooters with painted faces and the dumb beasts drinking their fill at the mashed edges of the black pit.

So our first hypothesis, that we had discovered a body made frantic with some enviable ecstasy—a belief naively enhanced by our seeing it anointed with a beautiful visage, a beatific state of preservation—was brutally supplanted by the image of undying agony, dancing devilishly in the mind's eye of our most scientific knowledge of the facts. The facts are never very far from the fears that haunt our love of beauty, are they? And don't we need to do the ugliest things in our own defense?

So this is what makes me consider more empathically the poetic injustice of our Taste's professional fate: to begin his career in a place where the fruit of daily labor is always a more pained knowledge of the cruelties that apply to human flesh. It could only have a more damaging impact on a sensibility already so bruised by the memory of violence.

Is it too droll of me to surmise that in his case a perfect memory is too much of a good thing?

Punishment is of course its own memorial stone. Time passes, but the violent act perseveres with granite determination, indifferent to the forces of erosion that prey upon the soft tissue of our mortal pleasure. Places like the heath are evidence enough of what remains, of what time preserves in its memory.

So I was not unmoved by Roscoe Taste's predicament; the daily recollection of his childhood pain that we unwittingly collected from this prosecutorial plot of land, like a harvest of personal grievances for him to ruminate over. His very vocation had turned on him like any sickening organ of the body.

"If only one were not oneself!" it makes the victim cry out.

And wouldn't we sympathize with anyone who sings this complaint? Anyone whose voice still quavers with the reverberations of a violent blow?

But there are other considerations. We mustn't forget that the mark of Cain is a wild spore. It endures where it spreads. The suffering child becomes the punishing adult with a perverse alacrity. The annals of this perversion are legion in the record rooms of our hand-wringing psychiatric experts. Does it not give us some dreadful pause to consider this fact?

For all that I forget—I admit it even in this crystalline-as-a-teardrop moment of remission—it seems I must remind you that the violence of which we are speaking here and now was perpetrated against the woman I loved. Who loved me back. Who therefore deserves this reciprocity of my strong feeling. I speak of the crime at hand. Lest we forget. I speak of the specimen because it may remind you of the crime that you are charged to solve, even in your most disrespectful questions to me.

So I will not shrink from saying what I feel.

For all the professed innocence of this Taste's victimization, we cannot shirk the suspicion that he carries the spore of the victimizer in all the feverishly replicating cells of his being. Nowhere more virulently, I will hazard a guess, than on the viscous, humid, mildly enflamed surface of his tongue. I might even say you are already the victim of his speech.

Even if I were his father—you can't deny that the finger of his accusation points, however waveringly, in my direction—I could not let my natural sympathies stand protectively in the way of a higher duty to the truth, however painfully it might be inflicted upon me. I must lay the facts bare, however painful to us all. Is there anyone who eludes the black lash of suffering in this life?

Is there anyone who goes unpunished?

Since Dundeed brings us to the corpse, let's not stumble over it. Let's be assured of a thorough examination of all the evidence that is exhibited in the extraordinary clear sightedness of *rigor mortis*. And let's not be distracted by our affections, real or imagined.

You found her in a furrow of the road that leads to Dundeed's manse—that borders the find site—as if she were a pilgrim who had perished along the way of an arduous devotion. Wouldn't he flatter himself to think so?

She lay instead like the mortal flesh ravished by divine revelation, the open eyes struck heavenward by the blow of the shovel. Glittering eyes of a doll, flashed open by the snap of the wrist required to pull the head apart from the narrow torso.

She was dressed for the dig. Dressed like him, in ridiculously pouffed jodhpurs. Hobnail boots laced to the knee. The trademark pith helmet lying like a mercilessly overturned turtle not a foot from the open hand, still outstretched in some accusatory gesture toward the red brick roadway that rode above her head.

How like a barrow is a furrow, you have to admit.

And weren't we meant to find her as if she were something freshly dug out of the earth rather than dropped contemptuously into one of its carelessly open doorways? Isn't this why the hacking shovel, the murder weapon—you yourself have confirmed it—was left so incriminatingly in the way of anyone who would discover her body?

As the one who discovered the body, even though you had already been tipped, even though a mysterious phone caller had shadowed my solitary footsteps without my knowing it, so that you were already on your way to the crime scene, your red and yellow lights and sirens alarmed to the chase, I believe I can say, with even more authority than the official investigators, what was the true condition of the body.

Dead, of course. But not just killed.

The body was arranged to tell something more than these brute facts of the case.

The blow of the shovel that had relocated her left profile to the ridge of her brow was all that was immediately obvious. But I had prepared myself for the worst—fearing her absence from bed, her absence from the trench, her absence from my arms—and so was poised to notice the subtler details of the scene.

It was a theatrical scene—make no mistake about it—and so the telltale handiwork of our maestro of muck. Don't I mean every disrespect.

For I saw how her legs were spread in no stance that could have been felled from mere walking. I saw the loose disarray of her breasts under the tightly buttoned tunic. The fly of the jodhpurs puckered open to reveal no trace of an undergarment. And there was certainly no ambiguity about the gold wedding band that had been brutally forced upon her already tumescent finger. The knuckle mangled after the fact to seal the permanence of the bond.

And what did you make of the lipstick—perfectly formed kisses—on her sleeve, on the back of her hand? Look closer and you will see it tracking from her elbow.

Which leads me to ask: why was the elbow so wretchedly twisted against the natural motion of the arm? The elbow does not break easily. Whose difficulty, then, do you imagine this was intended to be?

Now I think I must tell you exactly how intimate I have been with Kraft Dundeed myself.

I confess my own early ambition to be like him. Epigone if you like. Yet who would deny a young man his due naiveté? It is what proves our youth. I was that youth who aspired to professional renown. And he was the figure for modeling my clay.

But what probing fingers one needs to find the form of one's fate!

I flattered Kraft Dundeed by showing him the full and luminous depth of the true acolyte's heart: I revealed the most private details of my life. What more gratifying looking glass can be proffered than the one that reflects the power of judgment? What personal weaknesses and woes did I not parade to prove the worthiness of my submission to Kraft Dundeed's judgment? Thus did I earn the aptness of my appointment to his lead field team.

And not the least of the confidences I tendered was the tale of my mother's shattered elbows.

He knew. And it would not be lost on Kraft Dundeed that the crook of the arm is the nook of parental affection, where the hair is tousled, the kisses are planted. Didn't his predilection for playing the father figure with me signify nothing more than his desire to inveigle my head there, where all the leverage of the nutcracker could be brought to bear?

Kneeling over Cinna's lifeless body I felt the full force of it.

So you see, the garishly twisted arm, the broken elbow, were the set decorator's most exquisite touches. Details to lend the drama its perverse life.

And wasn't Dundeed at home when you identified the mystery caller? You did observe the wheelchair so foolishly parked by the phone. As if it were even needed. Was it the butler who answered the door?

But then you saw what he wanted you to see. Prisoner of the chair. Bundled in flannels against the damp, as if the bundle of his own bulk weren't warmth enough. You recall the helpless dangle of his feet from the chair. Unslippered, but plumped by their own woolen skins. How like an invalid he looks.

But you ignore the conspicuous detail. The feet dangle because the footrests have been folded out of the way for easier access to the seat.

Innocuous incidental? Or screaming telltale of the haste with which the lummox gamboled onto the stage, scurrying for his mark?

Innocent? Or guilty? It is your question to worry. Even though you think I am on the worrying end of the tether your inquiry tugs upon. I am patient for you to unravel the strands of this mystery on your own.

I am patient. Like any innocent party.

Patience in pursuit of truth is no virtue, I'm sure you'll agree, sitting for as long as you have between the two of us.

Perhaps I can hasten the process by convincing you that Cinna's *Theory of Old Men* is no theory.

I am an old man. But I am not buried in my years. I have been trying to persuade you that the years are the generous accretion of an ever more vibrant skin. And would you doubt any longer that Cinna is under that skin now, in fact a peachy hue of its impossibly youthful pallor? I can bring it out like a blush. With your help.

After all, the scraping of your chair against the floor, as if you could walk away from me on its shiny metal legs, brings back to me the salty pleasure of our—Cinna's and mine—most ardent sexual position: her legs straddling my thighs, the friction of our bodies—my flammable wick, her combustible oil—igniting the seat of that other wooden chair. I told you already. Remember?

You rise to your feet as if from the force of that combustion. I have to smile.

But your little conflagration is incidental to the livid ember of memory that I wish to fan into flame for you here and now.

With your compliance, please.

If you could reseat yourself as you were. If you could assume the attitude of skeptical disgust that had you grinding your chin into the palm of your hand a minute ago. If you would wash your head in the shadow of that blowing curtain and let its contours fall like waves of hair around your shoulders, then I might find a semblance of the woman who loved me. It would raise the hairs on the back of my neck. Perhaps yours.

Do you think you can you follow the tale? I can't tell it without you.

If you must know, it is your own nervous perspiration that gives away her presence to me here and now. The athletic body is really neither male nor female in its sweaty emanations. Though the scent of her was always an augury of her physical passion.

And this time was no exception.

She had sealed us off in the acrid wombspace of the Sanctuarium Scholasticus, had bolted the heavy wooden door, had coughed allergically into the clear light of her laughter, had taken her place in the life-sized mirror hung opposite the leather divan, had puffed out the loose front of her khaki tunic with a pillow from the divan.

She was performing a dumb-show mimicry of my professional self in the field.

With one quick hand she hoisted the red tresses off her shoulders and stuffed them into the snug bowl of the pith helmet. With the other she hefted the down-stuffed belly protruding under her tunic. She bent and straightened in a fast motion burlesque of strenuous shoveling, launching loads of imaginary dirt over one shoulder.

But her speech was the most remarkable effect of that antic cartoon. She filled the skin of my voice with the tentative roundedness of the breath stoppering a half inflated balloon. And yet, the authenticity of the timbre—she dug deep in her lungs for it—was exhilarating: *"the three d's of archeology, darkness, dampness, digging...the soft turds of time...born to the grave..."* I could have been myself there in the mirror, prating in her clothes, hugging her skin to my bones, feeling her flush openness between my legs.

But her laughter burst the balloon. She was doubled over with the convulsion. Her loose hair swept the top of her boots like the hem of a crimson gown.

"You know I meant no disrespect." She had swallowed the humor of the situation in a single alabaster gulp.

"I am your true epigone. I will prove it by becoming the medium of your magic spell."

For Cinna knew what I have been telling you all along: memory's proximity to the things of the present—the lascivious friction of one thing rubbing against another—is the only straight road to the past.

She was extending a nacreous hand from out of the mirror's hard gleam. Her purpose was that clear. She intended her arousing touch to be a conjuring of my sexual ghosts. The friction of two bodies would be fertile ground to forage for past lives. She was already trampling the pillow disguise that had fallen underfoot with the khaki tunic, the shucked jodhpurs. She was approaching on naked toes, no doubt imagining myself to be a mirror through which she could step forthrightly into the willowy arms of my past lovers. They were sister selves of the convolvulus motion of the hips that wedded her to her own time and space, as brazenly as the flame to the air it consumes. They might reach out to her. That is what she said.

We are not fools here either. The mirror in which we three watch our little drama unfold on the far wall of this very interrogation room looks both ways does it not? It looks both ways. And so it scintillates on the surface of my eyes with the knowledge of what she must have been searching for then. The secret eyes that are watching us, here and now, from behind that glass, know no less about it than she.

When Cinna was at last in my arms, I quickly understood it was her reach that mattered. Because she had reached beyond me. Her thickly bobbling chest and nuzzling pelvis, her melting tongue, had all been proffered to me as the titillating mnemonics of my youthful ardors. Like pictures in a flame, the bodies that had faded from my caress would flicker forth from Cinna's physical intensity, where she muscled it against me. She would prove her theory with her own body. Exactly what I have asked of you.

And now her blood was in the effort, coloring her face and limbs with the heat of the phantom heartbeats. And like the old man of her theory, I felt alive to their presences pulsing under her touch. All my past loves—so vividly did she conjure them—arose within me as I pulled her even closer. I felt myself hardening with the accumulation of those sifted grains of time, the density of one thing contained within another, where I stood more stolidly than ever, a more monumentally weighful presence than I had ever felt myself to be, even when seated at the escritoire of the Sanctuarium Scholasticus.

Even you would not have thought me so heavy as I felt then.

I needed your hand, you must know, to tell you so. Having pulled myself up by it until we are face to face like this—I really didn't mean to startle you, or topple you, though your pacing around my chair was a distraction that had to be halted—I have only mirrored the sensation that dredged through me then, of bodies being raised up inside me on the tensile strings of excitement that pulled from Cinna's silvery fingertips.

"Am I all the women you have ever loved?" And because she spoke with my fingers pressed against the small of her back—I can feel the pressure in the way you are pulling to extricate your fingers from the clutch of my generous palm—the low pitch of her voice might have been squeezed from the deepest hold of her being.

So I knew she was testing her *Theory of Old Men*. Testing this old man's gravity against her weightless longing.

Longing for what? Longing for what? I don't remember, you are not surprised to hear me say.

Then help me. Let me feel your breath on my eyes again and we might both understand better what she conjured from the cellular density of my old man's constitution. Time coagulating with the bloodiest sensations? Bodies in which my body became itself more palpably than anything I had ever touched with a hot finger?

When I lifted my eyes over her shoulder, and I peered again into the mirror from which she had so lightly tripped, I saw the pink animus in the dimple of her buttocks. She was finding the physiques of those other women in her own vortex of gyrations. Finding them for me.

For me. She was recalling me to myself, perhaps that there might be more of me for her. The look of disturbed waters in the mirror glass was my proof. For now I too was in motion, without thinking of it. I was adrift on a wild current of that water. I could end up anywhere.

For this willingness to 'go with the flow' she thanked me. I remember the quickening of her embrace, though your rude push, your stabbing hand, gives me backward steps. I cascade over them. The rocks in the wild current are its most seething knowledge of itself. But I land in my chair—you marvel at the shivering intactness of its spindled frame—convinced of her gratitude. For I am concussed against the wooden seat with the fullest weight of myself, and most resoundingly in the pelvic saddle where Cinna rode her most urgent purpose. There is so much of me here in this fallen state, that even you could honor her faith in the gravitational pull of larger bodies.

Surely you remember the cardinal precept of Cinna's theory. How could I forget, held as I am under the leaded glass paperweight of my own immobility: *The older man is his own place.* I could add, "The older man is his own place, with room for others.

"You are your own place more than ever," you want to chime in. "No one to sit beside you now, but nemesis himself."

And don't look at Taste. Look at me.

Don't waste your pity, if that is what you imagine makes you a better man than me. I move my arms. I bend my legs. And I can feel the strings tugging upon the other bodies. Awakened from their slack repose like dance steps tuned to the rhythm of my quickening pulse.

No doubt, in carnivals or music halls, you have seen the lonely dancers with their sheepishly attired manikins, fastened to their wrists and ankles by invisible wires. They clutch the moistened cloth hands in a perspiring whirl that blurs the breath between them. Every movement is doubled. Like writing on glass.

See me on that dance floor. My ungainly obesity—if you can't dislodge it from your judgmental eye—made miraculously svelte by the weightless lift of my partner. Cinna twirled me into this pirouette of sensations, where all my motions are forever accompanied. The living proof of her theory heaves in my heart against the breast of my partner. The dance never ends. And do you not see the affinity between Cinna's bodies and my bodies in the bog, which proves that we were soulmates after all? Partners in the dance that never ends.

And think of it. If you had not just pulled away, had not snatched your hand from my inviting grip, you might have fancied yourself my partner.

You, my partner at the policeman's ball.

No. I am ashamed to say that I am Dundeed's true epigone.

Of course, I saw him for the first time in the newspapers. His head swelled beneath the headlines even then:

ARCHEOLOGIST TURNS UP MUMMY EXECUTION SITE: DADDY OF DIGS!

I saw a younger man, strapped to a slimmer frame. But the head was already a prodigious portent of the girth to come. And holding his head up high in front of the camera like its own trophy, giving support to the bold face type that crowned the photo, he stood out from the gray and white porridge of Ben Day dots like something only covered in its pulpy sediment, not of it, breaching the surface of the photo emulsion, more real than any representation it could make of him.

Smiling, of course. But the smile, when I look back at it, was more than a sparkling sunbeam of the notoriety that illuminated Dundeed's career that day. Looking back on it, with what I know now, the sliver of crescent darkness scintillating between the curled lips—like nothing so much to my archeologist's eye as a bone piercing the crust of earth—bulges with unremembered significance. The lips that anyone else would imagine are drawing the first intoxicating breaths of his fame are disgorging something.

Could it have been anything else than the chewable word, the salubrious name that surely filled his mouth that day?

DIRTMOUTH.

No more propitious christening of a career in archeology was imaginable to me then. In the bottom right corner of the photograph—where Dundeed's left boot was severed from view—was a picture, framed within the picture, showing the discovery before she was carved out of the peat, still compressed in its footprint of time: the specimen itself was barely an outline against the marrowy pith of excavated turf. And yet, blurred as the image was with its grainy impress of ink and earth, the torsion of the body's suffering was vividly apparent to the empathic eye.

And do you not already know me as an empathetic soul, who would give even his enemy his due?

Years later I grasped Dundeed's hand for the first time with the sensation that I was being hauled from a sucking mire onto firm ground. Oblivious to the smear of newsprint that must have moistened my palm, I have no doubt. For didn't I imagine that I was still only an avid reader of his exploits? I might have pinched myself with the same fingers that had held the vellum pages apart making a taut trampoline for my focused breathing.

But here I was in the flesh. I joined the pose, stood beside him for the official inaugural picture of the find site that was ours together. First official commemoration of our discovery: HERMAPHRODITE HARRY. Beaming with all the light he needed for the picture, I followed the command of the news photographer's brusque hand gesture. Pressed closer to my idol. Squeezed more tightly into the frame. My ear brushed the great man's shoulder. The rustling of his shirtsleeve sounded like a word of encouragement to me, so giddy was I from inhaling the close air of those newsprint photographs through which I had followed his career over the years. That air was now drawn as tightly to the features of my camera-ready face as a plastic bag twisted over my head.

"Click," you might say.

From that moment I was frozen under the icy glare of the photograph in which you now see him standing beside me as in a glass box. Break the glass and you will hear the gulping breath of the nearly drowned.

Look behind the picture. Pry a view between the standing foreground figures, shoulders close as a row of teeth. Do not be distracted by my smile, which seems to be pulled by an invisible thread, tied to a crooked finger of the photographer's hand, and you will glean the slivered profile of a woman's face. Practically a blurring highlight in the picture. She too is peering out of the picture, beyond the frame. But she is looking in a different direction.

Let me tell you, Cinna's eyes were as sharp as your own in their detective dissection of the scene. That brightly photographed afternoon, with the sun fallen so deceptively like a shroud over her face, she was already moving towards the object of her gaze. Moving behind the eyes of the posed team leaders—ourselves blinded by the light of the occasion—she looks like nothing so much as an unconscious thought flitting through our collective heads.

But she was on a trajectory of discovery all her own at that moment. Squint more concentratedly and you can make out the determination on her face like something scratched into the emulsion of the photograph. See how she has caught and holds her bottom lip between her teeth.

I remember how the voice startled our picture out of its pose. Carried above our heads, like something cawing down on us, it turned our heads. And so the blur in the faces, the flaw in the picture, is the proof of what I am telling you here and now.

Cinna's surveying eye had dipped into a telltale declivity of the soggy bog patch that stood adjacent to the tented area of the site. It was an unusually large "birthmark" as Dundeed himself liked to call the depressions in the earth that portended discovery.

By the time we had struggled to stretch the rubber skins of our ditch boots over the brick shaped sidewalk shoes that had stood us so stolidly in front of the camera, Cinna had already cut a perimeter line with her spade. She had already traced a grid over the plotted ground with a six-foot length of scrap timber and the handle end of a rake.

The team arrived with all the clatter of a wooden-wheeled ox cart tethered to Dundeed's boot prints. He was holding his hand up. Signaling a halt. Signaling ahead of us.

It was the gesture of the orchestra leader banging on the last note of the last bar, as if it were the last nail in a coffin lid. He was his own flag planted momentously upon the terrain. Standing beside Cinna's shovel, as if to challenge its firmness. He had to step around it in order to have his way with her.

His heavy hand on Cinna's shoulder, his face suddenly close as the buzz of a mosquito to her rosy cheek, perhaps only close enough to secure a whisper, perhaps close enough to be nibbling her earlobe, he leaned into her, crowded her space. Silence ensued as if someone had filled in a hole. I knew from the sight of him shaking Cinna's hand that there was now a pact between them, though I had no scent of the intimacy he had sweated from her weaker grip.

This was to be my fault. You see, I can't be accused of shirking my responsibility. I had introduced Cinna to the great man out of my enthusiasm for *him* as well as for her. Wasn't I *his* suitor first? Little could I have known that between them—the nubile beauty and the hoary crag—my mind and body would be turned 180 degrees. Does it not sound like the unwilling bed partner in an aggrieved *ménage a trois*?

You would be wrong to think so.

I met Cinnabar McDermond for the first time in a bookstore.

My appointment letter to the new university expedition team beat officially in the breast pocket of my stalking coat. That headstrong pulse led my determined stride on the narrowing cobbled streets through which I hurried to perform the last-minute preparations for my professional novitiate. In two days I would be below ground, descending, my feet balancing on the rungs of time.

The bookstore specialized in physiognomy textbooks: ALL SPECIES.

Cinna's tall, limber frame was folded into a musty corner of shelving. Her eyes were lost to the blackened ceiling beams. Her hand, burrowing beneath one lapel of the houndstooth overcoat that draped her to the floor, was unmistakably massaging her left breast.

Not moaning. Not smiling. Looking straight at me, with flint-eyed determination.

I had dropped a fold-out page beneath my grasp of a volume on scalps and tresses. My eye was following a plaited length of raspberry locks indistinguishable from a woolen muff.

I had seen what I had seen. But I let the unfolded, dangling page be a screen of discretion, and buried my face in the must of the binding sutures that pierced my sinuses as sharply as the needle that had sewn them.

The book had been as shut to the air I could no longer breathe as the sheaf of meticulously combed hairs that hung before my eyes. Though detached from the head they "slept upon" (according to the legend at the bottom of the page), these "pictured tresses were as vibrant with the color of a burning flame as any dream cupped within the cranium itself."

Archeology is such an empurpled science.

Yet Cinna's words, suddenly flickering around the edges of the hanging page, licked the top of my skull with as fervent a flame.

She had recognized me—from my orange hair?—from my photo in the university gazette? The announcement of my election to the field?

But she spoke of Dundeed first. She came toward me, letting her hand fall from inside her greatcoat, extending it in my direction. Nippleless I had the wit to observe—of course not to her!—as an afterthought of the warmth nuzzling my palm.

With the formality of that handshake she straightaway solicited an introduction to Kraft Dundeed. As if I weren't there in any other capacity. As if I even knew him yet. As if I were his proper pimp.

"Of course," I replied, like the infant with the nipple stuffed between its teeth. Didn't I have to bite down on my tongue to tell this lie? Didn't I want her to smile, open lipped and moist, into the intimate precinct of our nodding heads? Didn't I want to close my mouth over her teeth?

In any case I gave her my word.

How good was my word then! Not a week had I passed with the archelogical team when she appeared for the oh so hollowly promised audience with Kraft Dundeed. My ears were still ringing with it.

Now *she* would have to be *my* first find. I would have to interest him in her more than myself, if I were to hold her interest in me.

At least she carried a parcel, a box trussed with yellow twine. Her long ivory fingers bore the weals of the knots. A specimen to barter for her boot print on the find site. I knew it even then. The archeologist is intuitively a trader because he knows better than the man who only sets foot on the surface of things, that what is trod beneath us will one day rise above us. He is the mire that drags upon his own step. For the impassioned archeologist one thing is always already becoming another.

She was attired for the field, and stamping her feet as if I had hired her, rather than lied to her. I spied over her shoulder through the glaring doorway of the tool shed—I had been assigned this morning to ready equipment for the day's excavation—to reassure myself of a moment of privacy. A rakishly tilted pith helmet showed the color of Cinna's hair like a match head scraping against the roughness of my anxious eye.

The pouf of her jodhpurs twitched on her flanks, a whisper in the air as tensile as the whisker of a cat. The litheness of the feline backbone made an unexpectedly sinuous action of her passing the parcel to me.

My hands seemed to buoy up, the package was so light. They fluttered to keep their grip.

She wished me to approve of the offering, to cut the strings, to unfold the brown waxed paper from the sharp corners of the wooden box. To declare its value.

It was of course the head that you have already heard tell of. My thumbs, hooked under the brazen cheekbones, lifted the item into the shadow-shedding light that flooded from a small barred window behind me.

Bronze age and worthy of a museum case. Not extraordinary as a specimen, except for the jigsaw pattern of fissure lines that webbed the fascia of the bone as intricately as the network of capillaries that might have blushed those high cheeks.

Jawless, staring down at me out of its darkly shafted sockets. I detected that it had once shattered into more pieces than could be cupped in the palm of one hand. It had been puzzled together with tweezers and a cement that will tear the skin from the working fingertips, if permitted to dry before the next shard can be grooved into place. It would have bristled with more edges than a searching finger can feel for before it begins to bleed. It was a masterpiece of reconstruction. And so it would be of no inconsiderable sentimental value to the unusually astute eye and hand. My open palm upon its forehead fevered with the fineness of the cement sutures that grained the calcareous surface.

And so you understand my dilemma. I asked myself. Should I play pander between this avid woman's professional ambition and the professional interest that this specimen might well titillate in the mind of Kraft Dundeed? Did I not feel a jealous bone stiffen, like a thrombosed artery in my heart, at the thought? My succor for her would be my forfeit of his esteem.

I watched the heave of her bosom under the khaki pocket flaps of her field shirt, felt the tip of my tongue like the remembered nipple caught between my teeth. Or was it the word I could not pucker to my lips: "Perfection."

Such an aesthetic judge I have always been.

But now I held my judgment back, waiting to see if she would ask again.

She only breathed out. Perfume of figs? Sensation was seeded in me like a ripening pith.

She took a step.

The next thing I knew, my own head was afloat in her caressing hands. Her long white fingers drew the slackness of my cheeks into blushing sinews.

I felt the drag of my feet beneath me like a sack of grain.

And then her lips, cool, full of trapped juices, rouged as the skin of the grape that mumbled between them—I thought I heard it speak—saturated my breath with their intoxicating slowness.

It was a kiss that lapped against my moorings. And when I felt them shift, I feared the worst.

Which head did I let drop? I have you guessing.

Mine was the head that plummeted from that kiss. She took the exquisitely reconstructed skull back into her naked grip, letting the wooden box fall between us. The box was as hard on my toes as the hammer upon the heads of the nails that held it together. I felt a stroke of the hammer hand swing in my recognition that she was not waiting for me to lead her into the field. She was already gone.

She had merely blinked, as if she were the one snapping out of the spell of that kiss—I might have merely been the cinder in her eye—and turned into a shaft of light that stolidly propped the door open to a view of the dig site: it shone most pointedly in the aluminum ladder descending to the quadranted ground terraced beneath it. The muffled sough of a lone pick biting into soft ground was all the sound that breathed into my ear.

I caught up with her at the bottom of the ladder. She was a bronze statue of purposefulness. Her hand, cocked against the gleam of the early morning sun, shivered the rim of the pith helmet. She seemed to pass all the grossly granulated field that was spread out before her through the thimble-sized sieve of her surveying eye. Spying Dundeed.

But before I could touch the rigid epaulet on her shoulder, she had come to life. The bronze statue became a molten flow and was as swiftly out of my reach. She had seen him. The oily knob of Kraft Dundeed's baldpate breached from furrowed ground ahead and shone like a blister under the intensity of the sun.

I felt my own footsteps cut short by the length of her scissoring stride. I might have been the perspiration between her legs—I must tell you that at a later time it beaded there as a distillation of my pleasure—I was so breathless to catch up.

I saw what troubled event I had set in motion by admitting Cinna to the find site. Hadn't I sworn myself to the protocol of the dig? "No visitors! No Exceptions! Our watchword is never!" So Dundeed had ordered it.

Wasn't she unmistakably my visitor, even if I was the one dragging upon her boot heel?

The infraction of the rule was already staining my clothes. Under the arms, across the chest, spreading from the crotch of my trousers.

And at this pace they would see her first. Coming up behind her, my breathlessness would give me away, if the map of my perspiration did not. I could already hear myself choking on the heartblood flooding my larynx.

Would she be so forthright as to speak for herself above the gurgle of my embarrassment?

I suddenly felt the answer to the question spring alive in my fingertips. Did I see them white-tipped with urgency? I saw her arrive at the brink of the five-foot trench, imagined the four surprised faces lifting out of the shadow she cast over them like a perversely discovering light, and knew that my hands would not be stopped in her tracks. My last three steps to catch her were freighted with a careening intent: to push her in.

But before I could lay hands upon my own shadow—wriggling up the small of her back like a spontaneous shiver down her spine—Cinna had jumped.

She had already jumped.

And I was left to catch my balance at the ungraded edge of the trench. I saw the ridiculous figure of a man throwing an armful of invisible snakes up into the air and trying to catch them one by one on their slithering return.

But of course no one noticed me.

When she landed in the pith of the trench, Cinna lost her grip on the fragile specimen she had so ceremoniously submitted to my inspection, which even the eye sockets gave no purchase on.

But Dundeed himself was the one to proclaim it a charmed accident.

Wasn't he the one who professed to hear—above the muscular thud of the woman's body plummeted onto his own stooping shoulders—the portentous clink of the shivering skull? In all the muffling fiber of the peat bog, only the blow of bone on bone makes a sound as clear as glass.

At both their feet, Dundeed's and Cinna's—how did they find their feet amid the tangle of limbs into which they had fallen?—the pointed shards of the broken skull, lying like a shattered crown, called everyone's attention to a fissure in the meticulously swept trench floor. Like a half opened eye, it shone with a bloodshot hue. But unmistakably skeletal. A facial bone. A proud cheek, turning into the light after a sleep of centuries. Only to be struck a blow—insult that would have rendered it a handful of fragments were it not still so deeply buried—violent enough to darken the windows of the soul.

What a rarity the coincidence of that glancing blow! What telepathy, one head finding another! Dundeed wished us to marvel at it, as though the clinking happenstance itself were the prize. As though the ringing moment in time were the real *find*, more precious than all the soundless years vaulted within the still unearthed bone. As though the present were more real than the past.

It gives me pause, the echo of that sound, though I never heard it then. Thinking back on it from this moment, I have to ask myself. Does it not ring a nearly inaudible note of truth from what our false witness—who sits ever more sullenly beside me—has so plaintively sworn? He scorns memory. And yet I have to remember (do *you* remember?) his words to say them: “The one who speaks to you *here and now* is the one who is most present.”

Who could that be?

× × × × ×

You can taste the venom in his words if you repeat them to yourself. Unalloyed bitterness, I'm sure you'll agree.

But I am not incapable of sympathizing with his dilemma. He has his mother to blame after all. I have found it in my book! Here, read it for yourself.

Is this Taste really the epigone I seek?

Today he brought his heart for me to touch it. I gave it one stiff-fingered prod and knew at once its inner flabbiness.

He says he loves a woman with red hair, the color that lit his mother's face. He wants to explain to me what he sees in her—as if I didn't know her well already—through the filter of redness, as it were. The mother I don't know at all.

And yet it is the mother he speaks of, with fiercely puckered lips to asseverate the words. He remembers himself as a feeble child, with silver braces cladding his skinny legs, and the clinking of the their hinged movements shadowing every footstep. Then how could he follow, as he tells it, his mother's soft-padded elopement from the house in the most hushed hour of the night?

And weren't there steps to descend the porch?

The satin yellow sheen of her back was all the shimmer to guide his movements in the windblown darkness. The laced hem of her gown left a visible wake on the heels of her naked feet. He had to follow closely or she would have vanished like a fish furled in the undulation of a darker depth.

Of course, the wind must have covered the rattle of his tracks. Woman and child passed through a nearby stand of trees, its familiarity shredded by the buffeting of the wind. And because they walked with the wind the boy didn't realize they were moving in the direction of the coops.

The chickens all asleep at that hour. But the wind was pecking his ears, burning his eyes as tearfully as the acrid guano of the hens, when he dragged his feet through the straw. So, his surprise to see the moonlit vane—silhouette of a rooster raising Gabriel's trumpet to his beak, and veritably crowing with the agitation of the weather—was doubly confusing for its aptness.

But his mother was not moving toward the crib grate. She was not, as he imagined, afloat in a somnambulistic dream of feeding the chickens. Her purpose quickened in the direction of a shed that stood apart. A workman's makeshift domicile, though the boy knew it breathed with the same fetid air that ventilated through the beaks of the sleeping chickens.

The searchlight beam that suddenly flared from the open door checked the boy's advance.

He could see the moonlight fluttering the wings that were his mother's naked shoulder blades. Though he had been riding the flicker of her bare back all this way, enhancing his sense of the weightlessness of the pursuit, he knew he would not be able to follow her aloft, where the wings would take her from this point. He felt his legs go as cold as the steel braces that gripped his step. Then, as she stepped into the cone of light—it pointed in the direction of her toes—the boy realized his own stark visibility, frozen not ten yards behind her. He was standing in the open, and etched as clearly by the stylus of light, as his mother's silhouette.

Because, in the twinkling source of the light, he could make out an equally dark figure, shadow of the hand that propped the door open. Though his mother's lithe form swooned in the direction of the door, the boy knew that the man—he could already see the perspiration silvering the naked chest—the man, shedding light with every step, was coming for him. Coming quickly, and with a dreadful arm outstretched in the gesture of the falling axe. The boy had seen the heads of the chickens spring openbeaked after their shocking fall. Nothing came from his mouth either.

With the man's crooked arm clenching him under the chin, the boy felt the breath of chicken feces hot upon his face. The light from the door was already throbbing in his head, though his eyes were pinched shut in the struggle to be free. He felt his heels dragging against the rocky ground in the direction of the door. The rough passage rang hysterical notes from the untuned metal of his braces.

Inside the small, harshly lit storeroom, the boy observed a rough table awash with a green hue that shone from the empty bottles littering its surface, a chair, its back broken away from the caned seating, the unkempt mattress on the floor. It bore a stain like a hole bored into its very center. The sheets were grimed with boot prints. The planked floor was littered with a poppy-seed-like grain that made the man's boots sound like roller skates when he moved.

He had the boy by the scruff, but his words were spewed at the woman. The mother's flaming hair flailed in the boy's face as she leapt to break the man's grip. He shouted in a voice the boy at first mistook for the scrape of a clawed furniture leg against the gritty floor.

The boy remembers the concussion of the word he had never heard before, though it shamed him as red as if he had awakened again from the dream of his nakedness before the other children at school: "Then you'll let me be the one to pay? Careless cunt."

And the boy felt himself fly free. But it was his mother whom he saw twisting away from the brutal entanglement, as if the man had pulled the string on a colored top rather than swung his rose-knuckled fist at the place where her eye had gone dead white.

She was abruptly seated upon the floor, against the wall where she had struck her head. All her joints were loosened by the impact. Her legs splayed out in front of her like sticks broken from a tightly fastened bundle. The color in her hair seemed to have emulsified where the boy saw her daubing her cheek with her unbroken hand. The boy could see the other, turned backwards on the trembling wrist. It was something done by stern-faced children to hapless dolls.

Then this Taste said the oddest thing: that he liked the way her hair looked like blood on his hands—his fingers combing through it—because it wiped off so pristinely from the papery whiteness of her skin, by which, of course, I realized he meant the younger woman. The one for whom his love was a disturbance that only my advice could calm.

He never knew how to flatter me!

But I gave him my advice today. I told him to worry a bit more concertedly about the habit he has of confusing one thing with another. I warned him of the damage one can do should he forget that love always begins with one's own self. And if he was in trouble with love he should try looking backwards out of the mirror. Practice the inward stare.

But he demurred. And that is how I begin to understand him. He asked me to consider that the woman's hair is red. Her eyes are green. The first time he saw her they cast a green light that made him gasp. And then he was swallowing seawater. Salt in his eyes. Salt in his stomach. His legs lost to him as when he was a child struggling to steady the crutches in the tender pits of his arms. He asked her to stand still so he wouldn't fall.

He had followed her into a bookstore. They stood amidst tall shelves and teetering stacks. A high diamond-shaped window—utterly out of reach—shed a squalid light that blurred the air and barely outshone a shaded wall sconce in the shape of a shell. He stumbled against an invisible shoal of piled magazines on the floor. In his fall, Taste had inadvertently thrust his hand inside her greatcoat and caught himself on her breast. She only breathed more heavily into his wilting palm. And when he had a grip of himself, so that he might remove the hand with some pained grace, she reached for it with her free hand and shook it properly, even vigorously he had thought. The red hair flamed in front of his face to flush him more deeply than his shame.

"Cinnabar, Cinnabar McDermond" was the introduction she proffered.

He accepted and walked her to a nearby tearoom where he watched her face to see if the passage under a new light had washed away the resemblance that had so smitten him. Even the light rain that had matted their hair and muddied their footsteps did not smear the conviction of his judgmental eye.

It gave him courage to towel her hair with the embroidered napkin from her own lap without asking did she mind. He poured her tea and smiled to see her green eyes, her lips, her nose, not to mention the still sodden red hair, reappear unsmudged from the cloud of steam which he had flourished over her tinkling cup like a magician's cheap stage prop.

In the dregs of the tea he augured the reason to invite her to his rooms—however disarranged by his packing—where he imagined that his photo albums awaited a reckoning with fate. He only wanted her to look with him. He only wanted her to see.

But he didn't want to sit beside her on the old chesterfield when she cracked the binding of the album, levered the album cover, the black boot-leather sheen of which showed you your face, if you could resist the desire to look inside. Taste tells me that Cinna did not hesitate to put her hand inside, to finger the waxed paper interleaves, feathering the edges of the glassine windows. Through those windows, so he said, you watch time fall like a final snow.

And, of course, he didn't want to sit beside her because he preferred to see her through the focal length of his strong faith that when she came upon the photograph, as he knew she must, she would catch herself as surely as anyone passing a mirror in a hallway. While Cinna turned the pages, Taste squatted on the geometric convolutions of the oriental carpet, hugging his knees, rocking on his boot heels, until he saw the stoniness come over her face, as chill and gray and granular as the spell of the medusa.

When he lifted her motionless hand from the nacreous gleam of the page, it was satisfyingly cold to his touch.

When she asked him who the woman in the photographs could be, he says he kissed her hand and motioned, with the corner of his widening smile—he thinks of love on the trajectory of cupid darts—toward the bedroom door.

If only to stifle my own hilarity when he put it that way, I had to ask myself, under the deadpan mask of my attentiveness—

"Did she laugh?"—with all the boisterous breath I'm strangling now.

But Taste was grim-lipped to continue.

Because Cinna touched his face, held it. She moved closer, the features of her blurry countenance swept his eyes, nose, lips, chin, as delicately as a stroke of the sable brush. He felt the heat of her dilated nostrils in his ears, imagined, I'm sure, the passageways opening into the incubating womb space of her consciousness, vaulted, illuminated to a shadowless round, hovering with the warmth of her thoughts of him.

She was moving still. He felt her lips feather against the high color of his cheek, the breath of tongue slithering, and what was surely the playful grip of the bared teeth. The thought of that playfulness was like a piece of loosely hanging garment swaying into the meshes of a whirring machine, before he sensed the muscles in her jaw tensing and the levers of bone gave brittle, jagged, points to her teeth. They had already cut through the taut pastry of his cheek when he realized it.

Tasting blood, he nevertheless knew he could not recoil, could not tremble his lips to cry out. He could only bite down himself, gritting his patience, until Cinna deliberated upon the terms of his release. And when she did release him, it was onto a short leash of words:

"Then that will be your birthmark," she purred, and with a sinuous movement of her wrist, wended her hand between his legs, as if to pleasure the pain with paradox as, I can only speculate, was her more than vengeful design.

Because Taste, by his own account, did not question her motives. For him it was the much easier thing to accept a difficult birth, especially if it meant Cinna had acquiesced to the face in the photograph, the mantle of motherhood which he himself must have imagined, he had thereby inveigled her to put on. I am interpreting, of course. Because Taste said nothing of what it meant. Only the red of her hair, the blinking green eyes, the white hand that drained the blood from the body squirming inside his clothes. These were all the considerations he could compass in asking me to render an opinion.

Should he involve himself with a woman whose lips curled so distinctly like his mother's?

"Smile or frown?" I queried.

And then he had the temerity to say that he was asking because I am the age of his grandfather, had the man lived, and must know what women are like. "From memory," I have no doubt he intended to say! No doubt at all.

How curious that here in my book, and well astride of my pen, I am committing Roscoe Taste's mortal love to memory, while the ever momentous object of his affection impatiently awaits my visitation to her rooms, as unbeknownst to him as the most malignant forgetfulness.

FIELD INVENTORY: (September, 1995) Specimen #33, Crate #21

Male, of indeterminate age. If fully extended, the specimen would measure 1 meter, 50 centimeters. Anatomically indecipherable except for the back of the head, the shoulders and buttocks. Naked except for a leather cap, belt, and one moccasin-like foot covering, laced halfway up the calf. The length of the specimen is warped to the embrace of a large, eviscerated dog. Bigger than a contemporary wolfhound, but hairless. Shaved with an extremely fine blade, of which there is no other record or specimen example. No valid speculation.

Found lying on his side and so tightly clenched to the body of the dog that the human epidermis is sutured to the animal, perhaps by the leeching of natural elements. Insertion of the scalpel blade releases a silicon-like granule.

Evidence of evergreen forest—needles, mulched bark, tarry loam—lodged between the toe-pads of the dog. The unshod human foot is calloused but clean.

Here I must impart a personal observation: am I alone in wondering if we do not defraud the specimen of its authenticity to inventory it in such smugly taciturn descriptive particulars? As if our reticence to state more than we observe were itself a form of knowing?

Women of science ought to know better. Our bodies candidly tell us that whatever is will be something else. Nothing stays the same. Even in the deoxygenated pressure chamber of the thousand-year night.

Haven't I answered this question to your satisfaction? By now you should be able to envision—by your own lights—what violence the man is capable of, notwithstanding the obesity of his malice, notwithstanding the decrepitude of the feral will.

You could ask Mr. Levant Doyle. If you could find him. You'll have to dig a bit, mind. So we'll make a proper archeologist out of you yet, since mere detection will obviously never suffice.

You've heard of his museum, certainly. But I need to tell you more.

Mr. Levant Doyle was more than a ribbon cutter. Oh yes. He wielded the christening shears—gilded by a burst of the photographer's flash—as momentously as if he were presiding over a throbbing umbilicus. With the opening of each new gallery of his museum, Mr. Levant Doyle appeared as master of a ceremony that might have required the donning of black robes and hoods, the choral chanting of ritual-shrouded words—to judge by the stentorian resonance of his elocution and the pontifical flourish of his hand gestures. But he was more than a ribbon cutter.

Finance was his official domain. A charitable giver, a patron of science. His benefactoring was his sole endearment to Dundeed. A man, a museum. What greater manifestation of human worth could Dundeed conceive? But you had to see them together to fully grasp how one man took his pleasure with the other.

It was Dundeed who claimed to know Doyle for what he truly was: "...a morgue thespian! Another one from the world of the living—far—too—well. For them archeological find sites are little more than the wings where one bustles into one's face paint and costuming, swooning for one's rendezvous with the spotlight."

Didn't I spy them—Dundeed and Doyle—in the wings?

Both together. And I thought: crowding one another's rehearsal space. Prologue to unveiling the Gallery of the Horse. It was an event for the invited press.

Of course, I saw them at a distance. Mr. Levant Doyle was leveling the twinkling tip of his silver walking stick at the meridian of Dundeed's ballooning gut. Dundeed, raised unsteadily onto his toes, held a finger in the air above his head as if testing the currents. The words, flying between them like birds at night, were rendered inaudible by the faintly metallic hubbub of the waiting crowd of photographers and journalists who filled the rotunda where I stood, anticipating a commencement of the ceremonies. But my view through the Palladian corridor that connected with the new gallery—cordoned off with plush ribbon for the inauguration—was dramatically backlit. The glow effused from the several exhibit cases beyond, like a fog curling up the silhouetted legs of the protagonistic figures, who might have been carved on glass, who now faced each other with surprisingly courtly gestures, like dance partners consenting to a minuet. It was a gnomic tableau, until I realized the dance that joined their bodies was fisted with rabid blood and, apart from the mere physical violence, threatened the destruction of the exhibit.

Did I dare risk an exhibition of my alarm, by rushing into the footlights of this altercation, thus drawing the cameras to the very spectacle that my own eyes assured me should not be seen? My feet stuck to the floor. I was like some uncarved remainder of raw stone, still impacted in the quarry space from which the polished rounds of *perlino rosato* I stood upon, had been extracted. My awareness of the resonance of the hall rang through my bones like some telepathy of the virtues of stillness the stone knows best.

I stood quite stiffly still. I merely narrowed my sights, like the subtly furred iris closing softly around a silent film image, to focus the view as if it were mine alone. And so far it was.

The fat man moved unexpectedly, with the untethered lightness and erratic litheness of the balloon that mocks his physique. The dandy held his ground. At first they were only pushing. Doyle's sealskin bowler came off the top of his head, like the loosely fastened cap of an aggressively squeezed tube of ointment. Dundeed seemed to hover on invisible wires. Again the silhouetted figures danced back and forth across the screen of light still emanating from out of the recesses of the invisible exhibit cases.

And still my bobbling iris-eye view was strictly my own. Apparently the action was telescoped far enough down the protected hallway that if your own "looking" weren't fitted with the sliding focal rings of an ever-magnifying attentiveness, you wouldn't see. I could easily have collapsed the tubes of the telescopic eye into their brass casings and, steering my gaze away from the troubled line of sight, pointed everyone's attention in another direction. The rotunda was now full and brimming with an excitement that, for the moment, was its own distraction. I could have raised my voice above the tidal sounds of the voluble crowd and channeled their conviviality through another corridor of museum space, where the flow of their impatience might be more easily contained.

I did nothing.

I watched. I was absorbed. I was a private audience in the thrall of the peepshow.

I might even have unconsciously shrugged a hand off my shoulder, brushed off a tug at my sleeve. For a moment, I was oblivious to everything but what I saw.

And there, in the snug and sound-proofed cabinet of my engrossed eye, the crime was committed. What I'd witnessed to this moment, despite its portent of a public relations disaster, was light comedy, however furtively malevolent the intent of either or both of the foolish antagonists may have been. They no doubt quarreled over who would speak first or longest before the audience gathering itself so decorously under the babbling marble dome of the rotunda. Pushing and shoving. A vaudevillian duo of forever-squabbling adolescent brothers or cousins.

Then: Doyle, stooping to retrieve his bowler from the short distance the fat man had kicked it, was caught under the chin, as though Dundeed had kicked the hat only to give the foot a better vantage for this blow. A swift and savage kick, aimed at the Adam's apple, sharp as a blade. It ran through me as coldly as if he had been a real assassin, throwing off the disguise of the actor on some unbeknownst stage of history.

Doyle reached for his throat like a man trying to hang onto his hat in a sudden gust of wind.

The gurgle that filled my ears must have sounded from my own throat. I was seized with a speechlessness as furious as the withdrawing foot, on which, in a miraculous moment, this most ungainly of men fairly pirouetted into a posture of perverse solicitude before his victim. As gracefully as a bird settling onto its roost, Kraft Dundeed knelt in front of Doyle on one knee, drawing the injured head into his open hands and bestowed what looked like a solemn benediction or a languorous kiss upon the whitening nape of the victim's neck.

He had kicked and knelt in one continuous motion, as sinuous and satin as the sheen of an ingénue's leotard. And because no sound of suffering, audible above the din of the unwitting crowd, marred the silent harmonies of that balletic imagery, I could have accepted it from my opera glass perch as a "beautiful performance." If I didn't know better. I know better.

I am no feckless aesthete. I'll stand on no beautiful ceremonies, as this more than venereal prick would have you surmise. Porcine cocksucker. Knobbling plonker. Mandarin head-fucker. Back-scuttling felch belcher. Pillar of piss. Gormless lunch box sniffer. Fart-mouthed blowhard. Haven't I admitted to a dirty mouth?

Even so, I'll warn you now, I'm no match for the filth that coagulates in the septic tank of Mr. Kraft Dundeed's high mind. I'll call him a high shite for decency's sake.

When I did, at last, step over the heads of the impatiently milling crowd, ascended to the raised dais that had been readied for other speakers, with chairs and lectern, a microphone dangling on a silver wire, when I stood alone to announce the regrettable cancellation of the long overdue event, I of course took care that the electric current, pulsing into the efflorescent walls of the still unchristened gallery, was extinguished behind me.

Later, after the crowd had decamped and I had secured the doors against any further intrusion, the scene was all too brightly lit. Though his throat wore a band of purple as tight as a corset, from the root of his chin to the swollen knot of his Adam's apple, Mr. Levant Doyle professed no injury. The breathy words hissed as if they were escaping from a hole in his neck. Though barely afloat on watery legs, he insisted on using his silver stick to attain the nearest chair. The sealskin bowler was back on the crown of his head, if slightly mashed. The fob chain swung like a frantic metronome from its buttonhole in the gold-striped vest. In a loosely hanging shadow, the fat man stood by, as if out of the most condescending respect for Doyle's stubborn will—his standing up in the shattered physique when it should have been lying down. Standing himself between Doyle and the chair, Dundeed only held out his hand as though he were leading a horse with a palmful of sugar.

No doubt, Dundeed will say he had his reasons.

I have said Mr. Levant Doyle was more than a ribbon cutter. For that reason alone you might imagine Kraft Dundeed's temper to have been short.

But then imagine more how Doyle crowded the stage: the incessant tapping of the silver stick on the floor as he scrutinized the weekly inventory, the finger forever pointing in a book to an item that the "maestro" might elucidate for the enthusiastic amateur, the litany of advice about architecture, the interminable raising and renovation of the museum building. Hear the shrill voice echoing through the exhibit halls, buzzing around the lugubrious hubbub of the guest parties Doyle led on weekly tours, retinues of investors, delegations of city leaders from Cork and Limmerick, blanche-faced teachers and students from the impoverished Dublin schools he patronized. The architecture seemed to have been deviously inspired so that the buzz of his voice recirculated through the halls to the central rotunda like an excitable pulse. Or as Dundeed would have it: "like a fly herding the death moans of a lost beast, sucked to the marrow of bog water."

If not a phrase-maker, always a morbidifier.

I point these things out not to excuse Dundeed's behavior, but to crystallize it with motive. You may extend your hand beyond the velvet rope of the exhibit to touch the motive and it will be as hard and smooth as any time-polished bone.

I'll set a scene—from memory of course—for you to contemplate on your own.

See the two of them in the field. Watch the way Dundeed walks the length of the trench with Doyle dogging his ponderous waddle. Do you doubt Doyle's lips are moving? Do you wonder that the long-handled spade cocked over Dundeed's shoulder is heart-shaped to make a highly specialized cut in the turf? Only their heads and shoulders are visible above the trench line. The black bowler follows the blazing baldpate like a snuffer after a guttering flame.

I am a fortuitous witness. My duty this end of day was to survey the gridded quadrants. To sweep them of unlooked for debris: the still perspiring bandana impatiently loosed from a parched throat, the errant hand tool that will be missed from the inventory of a torn cargo pocket, a detached boot-heel, a gum wrapper, a bottle cap, a fingernail. All the sedimentation of our workday that must be daily erased from the ledger of time, if we are to pick our way through the dirt without burying ourselves in the process.

Of course you can see Dundeed stopping in his tracks, like a man in mid-sentence slapping the sting of a mosquito on an already flush cheek. But because you know that Doyle lags four paces behind him, so that an abrupt halt on Dundeed's part subtracts precisely two paces from the space dividing them—measurable along the length of the spade handle—you know there is nothing impromptu about it. You can see.

Without looking, Dundeed snaps the smallest bones in his wrist, where they are levered against his grip on the nib of the spade handle and, torquing the action with a severe quarter turn of his shoulders, he is absolutely certain that the metal blade of the shovel will ring against the hard profile of Doyle's amazement, as incisively as the face stamped on a newly minted coin. The head barely wobbles before the body falls away beneath its sad tilt.

The shovel swings back across Dundeed's shoulders without even a swishing sound to tell what has transpired.

So perhaps it is more than mere motive I have crystallized by the words of my testimonial. However invited these attacks on Mr. Levant Doyle, don't we now know something of Kraft Dundeed that no sophistry of causation can confute: that the vicious nature of the acts reveals the person to be vicious in himself?

In which case the motive is in him like the sting of the honeybee, clutched so tightly within the golden muscle of the abdomen that the slightest rubbing against it draws the venomous point like a spasmodic discharge. Unlike the worker bee who suffers an abdominal rupture to plant the sting in its victim, the thrust of the angry barb makes Kraft Dundeed all the stronger. Run your warm hands, open palmed, over the smooth surface of Cinna's cold body and, cold as it is, you may feel for the minute snag of the stinger like a raised hair, or a splinter that has entered the skin in the form of an unwipeable stain.

I call it pastoral. Say it. The word sucks the past to its sibilant grain, as soggily as the kiss of bogmeal fastens on the bodies held in its dank keep. But you would be wrong to imagine that their day is past.

Pastoral is no sentimental lament for the past in this place.

I say pastoral. But where, you will implore me, are the green trees, the lambent grasses scintillated by the breeze, the birdsong that sweetens the already honeyed air with its staccato sugars, freshly sucked from the blossoms, the blossoms twining around stalwart trunks, whose colors make the light seem prismatic and the air to tremble with the thickness of the light, as if we were wrapped within it, chrysalides ourselves, luxuriating in the fermentation of our most colorful existence, which will bloom no less spectacularly than the wild rose, if our patience preserves us? Who are we kidding?

This place tells the truth. Bog. And it says what it has to say in a single ravenous syllable. Here all vegetation is ingestion. I do insist that the brown grain of the land is as dense as any towering trunk. The heather as tensile as any budding leaf. Its purple flower as fragrant as any footstep in the springing meadow. But none of it titillates our yearning for the picturesque.

The bog knows—as if to remind us how much better we should know this about ourselves—that its nature is not green.

Only remember how it came to be a bog. How like a murder. Almost eight thousand years before we gasp for our own breath. There was the fecundity of the lakes deposited like spawn of the retreating glaciers. The arrival of the Mesolithic fisherman. The reed communities. Their sediment, piling from the lake bed, poorly decomposed, the ground raising its dry hump, until only a few bubbles of lake water appear on the surface of the land. The water table rises with the landscape, gloomily acidic, airless, choking off the process of decomposition, until its lungs are full and blue.

Trees of the forest, fabled in birdsong, have spread their shadows over this ground. We find perfectly preserved specimens of them from when a drier climate cast its golden seeds of light upon the blackest humus. But when the damp returned—was it only a thousand years ago?—the oak, the elm, the ash were toppled by that tide. The thick mats of brown mosses took their places, an atavistic, pubic fur sprouting on the burly hump of peat. The dome of undecomposing earth. Ever rising, ever arching, feeding gluttonously on the indigestible midden of the fallen forest, and only at its edges, leeching out the iron rich ochre like ingrown maidenhead.

Bogdom. And the rulers of this domain today are princes of exhumation. But their faces, painted with the ochre so long ago, do not disguise their pathos.

Think of it. From the time of the first souring rise of the water table, the last days of the reed communities, when the wooly headed fishermen marveled at the miraculous appearance of land in the midst of waters that had hitherto only reflected their hungry, their dirty faces, this has always, always, been a place of punishment.

Yes, there are other pastorals. I have admitted it. They lie soft and green at our feet, but as far away from us as any distant valley. Only a leap into thin air—the sensation of shredded wings whistling about our shoulder blades—would bring us to that paradisal homeland. No. I think here we are closer to home, just because we are closer to the condition of punishment. Because here our pastoral is no mere ethereal dream of eternity. Here the uncompostable fact marks our time. Where decomposition has ceased, the composition of the natural world becomes more undecipherable than a human scrawl on the bark of a primeval forest. That is the end of any yearning to be green. The bodies in the bog are neither one thing nor the other, are they? Neither nature nor culture. You might even say the natural and the human are blessedly unknown to one another when they so densely embody the haste of time. I'm telling you, the bodies in the bog endure without any yearning at all. Do you know any pastoral as unsentimental as that?

Think of it. The hump of dry land having risen leviathan-like from still water. Maybe 1500 B.C. Visible but not approachable. Ringed with the feral tide of acid waters that sucks malevolently at trepidatious footsteps, the natural wonder of the bog-dome draws a helplessly introspective congregation. Who would doubt that it could stir the deoxygenated depths of some religious feeling?

Think of the throngs gathering at the water's edge, with each step feeling for the collapse of the earth beneath their feet. Think of the sensation tingling in their toes, the nails cracked and blackened as worn flints. They squish on the shrinking perimeter of the lake. These toes fringe wide, short feet, shod with calluses as impervious to the wet as gooseflesh, but attuned to the shallow immersion nonetheless. They know in their toes, as if the knowledge were an ingrown hair bristling toward the center of the brain, that as the water goes deeper it coagulates with the animus of something that can swallow hard. Everyone knows a bog to be a dangerous place. I tell you, the foot that fathoms such fear takes an initiate's plunge into the gurgling pool of prayer.

So, no sooner do the Mesolithic fishermen become Bronze Age farmers than the spongy domes of miraculously risen land—girdled as they are with waters chastened of any living organism—become sacred places. So, why should it surprise you to learn that, in the archeological record, the evidence of religious worship at these sites is indistinguishable from the rites of punishment?

I am the archeologist. I say so.

For centuries on, the congregants gather at the lip of this embittered shore. See the tall, Viking-framed priests, lifting long arms above their davening heads to stir the vapors of a settling mist. The reach of their arms sounds a clacking of wooden mallets above their heads. The glutinous weave of the robe material hangs shapelessly from their outstretched limbs, as though their entire bodies have been dipped in cooling oatmeal. Their eyes are coarse pits in the goat skulls that are lashed to their faces with leather thongs. They feel the pressure of the thong on the back of their heads like the grip of a violently forced kiss. But their lips are barely a cud, chewed in the wet, breathy recess of the snouted skull. Bowing their heads together they touch gnarled goat horns, like tapers passing a flame, igniting a sirenlike chant. It pierces the thickness of the settling damp. It whistles about the victim's naked body—of course she stands shivering in the center of their circle—like the biting end of a lash, primed against writhings of the very thin air from which the sufferer's first cries will burst at the commencement of torture.

But you would be wrong to expect such visual gratification.

The suffering of the victim will be invisible and relished all the more for its choked silence.

Oh yes, you can see her forced to kneel. The brutish hands pressing the delicate shoulders toward the wavering shoreline, where her knees are lapped by the ring of breathless water, blue as the face of a stillborn fetus. You can see the faces of the crowding spectators, eyes jostling for the better view of these priestly rites, hair stood on end with gouts of animal fat, cheeks streaked with ochre, tongues lurching against what might be the sound of words being ejected like a loathsome taste from the mouth.

And you can see her bound. The hands twisted like loose threads behind her back. Ankles lashed beneath the buttocks. A cord drawn, sharp as a blade, through the cleft of the buttocks, made taut along the spine, cinched tighter to fasten a noose around the neck. You can imagine how the struggle to free those limbs will be her self-strangulation.

And then you can even see the expression on her face change like windblown water itself. The fair skin, smoothed to translucent paleness by fright, suddenly wrinkling with rage. Watch the lines around the eyes and mouth whipping up a froth. And then the lips protrude in a wave action of their own.

You have no language to taste the meaning of these words on your own tongue. But you know the curses curdling on her lips, like the heaving of your own stomach. Think of the most bilious imprecation, meant to evoke the abject sullying of the mind in the filth of the body. You know the force of the tongue that wants nothing more than to smear the face, already stung by the breath of your hatefulness upon it, with the feces of the most bestially imagined bodily grunt. Who does not recognize how the angry contortions of the human mouth, when so vehemently aroused, are miming the savage extrusions of an animal anus? The word "shite" is no substitute for such knowledge.

You can see all that. And you can even see the helpless body being hurled out of priestly arms, beyond the ring of blue water, into the darkest fermentation of the bog.

But now you realize that your eyes have not enough light in them—even stoked by the incendiary sights burning there—to illuminate what follows. The weight of the body when it lands is felt by the victim like the very swallow reflex that has already throttled the screams in her throat. The slightest tremor of resistance to the clutch of mire quickens its peristaltic action and pulls her deeper into the gruel-like dark. A thin but grainy broth holds the compressed curds of deciduous plant life in curious suspension while she plummets in slow motion.

Imagine the blackness of the forest grave at night, darkened more blindingly by the furious footstep of time imprinted upon it. To be so trodden upon is her fate. For all the gloom you contemplate in your knowledge of this fact, you might then imagine that her eyes are closed. They are not. She stares belligerently at her foe.

And what is more appalling than those open eyes is the open mouth. She never ceased her cursing. For every mouthful of invective she disgorges, the tongue with which she whipped the air is forced to carry a lump of dirt inside her, to suffocate the thoughts that gave her oathing breath.

Silence beyond contemplation.

You think the violent moment has passed because you can see no more of it. You imagine the unimaginable to be like a hood pulled over your own head and the drawstring knotted about your throat. Perhaps, by the grace of this image, you are even relieved.

But this is pastoral, where nothing passes away.

When the tip of the spade unseals the airtight chamber from which the victim drew her last breath, in the form of an unswallowable clod, we know—I'm speaking for science now—that she is as undying as the leveled forest. It stands as tall on her tongue as she is compressed within it. All the bodies in the bog are creatures of this forest, if only by the corpuscular magic that renders them shriveled and sere. Sunlight and shade mottle them as thoroughly on the inside—should a blade be handy—as on the out. Their color is like the turning of the worm, passing through what it ingests. While the breeze that stirred every leaf is as tight-lipped now as the faces it might have sucked dry then, the flutter of birdsong, the golden buzzing of the bee, the silvery dart of the fly through that unremembered air, are all still sibilant in the squeaky texture of the turf, when we pry against it to unmold a shoulder or an elbow from the garmentlike fit of this land. It makes a sound against the cusp of the shovel blade like a loose floorboard. And it is explicable. For the remarkable compression of the elements of the forest floor—still bark flake and seed casing, still molted snake skin and dragonfly wing, still petal and frond—contains the spring of the very footstep that is blackened almost beyond recognition in the mummified foot filling its imprint. Root ball and bud are grown together in the dark. When we unearth them, the bodies from the bog are no less earthbound than the rocks and the stones.

What makes this specimen different from the others is that the spastic gash of her open mouth, still cursing, refusing to give up the grievance of a single moment in time, makes an itchy noise in our ears. It is our attunement to the fact that her endurance is our own experience of time. We will even mark it off in our faithful exhumation of the bodies, tendered by this otherwise unmerciful ground, in a state of such uncanny preservation.

And when we do cut them out of the turf, true to the minutest detail of what is preserved, don't we carry the tune of that cursing voice, as if we had picked it up from the lips of a comrade toiling rhythmically in the trench beside us? In the fields of excavation, we archeologists are laborers first, after all, spades and pitchforks wearying our calloused hands and our foreheads gilded with an honest sweat. If we hear the cursing voice are we not sworn, comrades in song, to be faithful to such harshly tuned rage, in all the ceaselessness of its expression?

When we close them in their glass museum cases we realize, as clearly as we can see through the glass, the transparency of time itself. Our victim's scourging tongue rings out on a resonant stage, if we have set the stage well.

How natural the scene! The arrangement of the limbs by means of invisible pins and wires floats the bodies in air just as they had rested—of course they struggled!—upon the peat. We see, between the splayed fingers, the light they are scratching to attain. We see the heads cocked on the straightened necks, the lips puckering towards the unforming bubble, on a surface beyond reach. We see the legs drawn up in the torsions of a frog propelling itself beyond the jaws of a cat, the hips knotted by a frenzied twist, wringing pond water from the air, toes pointing away like drops of water, shed from the density of the body. That we see them through the very air which denied them breath—the diastole of our inhale is the systole of their exhale—raises the pulse of our empathy.

Unlike the taunting rabble, long dispersed on the crumbling lake shore—they preferred the invisibility of the death because it more darkly bruised the blackness of their thoughts upon the victim's suffering—we, who have crossed the glaring threshold, bask in the footlights of the museum spectacle, knowing that it sees us as luminously as we see it. We feel the aching alertness of vision through such a limpid medium. The probing beams of light prickle the eye muscle as delicately as slivers of glass. The pupils are narrowed to steel pinpoints. The sheen of polished metal solders us to the view.

Staring ever harder with eyes that watch ever more closely—focus tensile as picture wire—we await the moment when, if only by the unsteadying blink of the eyelid itself, a limb will seem to twitch.

× × × × ×

Anyone who had witnessed Cinna bolting—so fleetingly fugitive—from Dundeed's Sanctuarium Scholasticus, would have harbored the same suspicion.

I squelched the knock in my fist and turned the knob. My leg, cocked at the knee, was as good as a crowbar. My mind was already raising the curtain on what I hoped to burst upon: Kraft Dundeed bent as helplessly as a man fallen into a well, struggling for a grip on his suspenders, force feeding the waistband of his trousers, beating down the frenzy of rebellious shirttails. The blood splashed in his face as shockingly as a bucket of iced water.

The titters and catcalls of the unruly audience were effervescing in my throat. I would have hurled a piece of fruit.

But the shock was mine to contend with. Dundeed was not alone.

And here was Mr. Levant Doyle. Not Cinna, as I had so blood-curdlingly hoped.

But you can't imagine a redder face, or eyes with as much to hide, however saucer wide. He was shirtless and somehow dripping with the exertion of an arduous swim. His breast still seemed to heave against a malevolent tide. He was bent over the familiar steel gurney upon which Dundeed always made his first inventory of the specimens that were ferried from the find site with the haste of a medical emergency.

Doyle's head was bowed under a medical headdress of sorts. A kind of elastic hatband, mounted with a Cyclops lens. A reflector light flickered behind it, as if the next breath might blow it out.

Had I ever seen Mr. Levant Doyle without his silver-tipped walking stick?

The platinum clasped monocle dangled on its chain against the unmistakably livid nipple of his breast, as if it too were straining to see something beyond the reach of an unmagnified fingertip.

The shadow of Kraft Dundeed, cast upon the wall behind his desk and spreading like a water stain as he extricated himself from the groaning chair, thwarted my focus.

My gaze, vacillating between the twin presences, made me feel the coarse threads in my neck twining together, preliminary to the threading of a needle or the baiting of a hook.

Dundeed twisted his lips into a barbed grin and crooked his finger.

No. I am not such a puckering fish as you imagine.

I used my feet. My leaner stride would carry me more quickly to the gurney than it would take Dundeed time to pirouette sidewise between the desk and the wall. How else would he even get into the race?

My flaming hand upon the gurney rail percolated the voice in both their throats with the abruptness of explosive laughter. In Dundeed's case it was laughter, but forced, I could tell. Pinched by the narrow passageway between the desk and the wall, the curlicued pitch of Dundeed's voice was more a pig's squeal than the low chuckle with which he no doubt meant to introduce a calming condescension to the frantic surprise of the moment.

I was already too well poised for inspection of the specimen—unusually long I noted—as I took in its tarry shape with a quick, feathery glance that, I later realized, barely touched the truth of it.

But I was not quicker than Doyle's fleet reach. With an unsuspected strength, he pried my fingers loose from the rail before I could steady my gaze. With his free hand he had drawn the canvas sheath from the foot of the carrying bed, to shroud the body in a rumpled blink of the eye. My fingers, where he touched me, were glazed with a stinging ichor, drops of which I noticed foaming, like a fierce peroxide, on the dirt floor at our feet. A tungsten filament seemed to flare in my nose, burning away the very odor that carried the sensation like its spore.

His grip still shackled to my wrist, Doyle dragged me against the motion of my own feet in the direction of his stranded partner, until he had a hold of Dundeed's hand as well and his own body wavered between us like a rippling sail, molested by two sides of the wind. In irons. Out of control. All the struggle, that heaved in my legs like a crew of sailors groaning at their winches, was of course unwittingly the lever to loosen Dundeed's boulder self from the narrow ravine in which he was lodged. I could only think, what avalanche must follow?

What I had not counted on was how far the pent up spring action of Dundeed's release from the wall would catapult me in the direction I desired to go.

With everyone jostled off balance for the moment, I purloined the leverage to free myself from Doyle's fist and turned the inertia of my body—however insecure the footing—back toward the gurney. My steps were veritable hops. I bounded against the hollow bones of the gurney, dislodging a clatterous tin that appeared to contain a licorice paste.

The canvas sheath seemed to be mottled with fingerprints from the contents of that tin as I bunched it within the hollow of my fist, and flourishing my forearm away from my body, I made a toreador gesture graceful enough to fling it over Doyle's approaching shadow.

The specter of Doyle's ghostliness struggling to throw off the sheath sent a shiver through my sense of what I had unmasked by the deftness of that throw.

"A third arm?"

I might have reached for it more quickly than I said it, before Dundeed rushed to untangle Doyle's furled head. It wagged as blindly as the tail of a yipping terrier.

But I was stopped by the stillness in Kraft Dundeed's voice. He didn't even move toward me. He didn't move, more than to stiffen his arm against Doyle's quavering presence beside him, subtly shortening his leash on the animal.

The extraneous limb, crooked at the elbow where a shard of bone had gnawed through the blackened crust of epidermis, its fingers electrified, prickled into full extension, lay diagonally across the deeply caved chest of the specimen on the gurney.

Had it borne a boulder? The collapse of the rib cage was the silhouette of something heaved against it as large and as round as that. I imagined the crushing weight as something torqued by the stone's flight through the air. A projectile. And a specimen with two arms of its own to defend itself.

But the extra arm was already in Dundeed's custody. How does the hand of a man so fat fly with such weightless agility? How does he shed his immobility with such gossamer ease? Now I could see that the arm wagged behind him like a bashful bouquet. The scribbling lips that were his nervous smile suddenly drew a straight line above his chin. He sucked in a breath like a lozenge that might dissolve on the tongue for hours.

I was left to stare into the specimen's sunken chest cavity, thinking that the hands, the texture and color of warming licorice, and folded piously athwart the genitals, had certainly not grappled with the violent projectile that had propelled him into gurgling mire.

But the other arm, now a jittery metronome in Dundeed's concealed grip—I could see the hand tick tock on either flank of the dapper sloth—was a better fit with the victim's fright, the breath routed from the lungs under the rushing shadow of the blow to the chest. For the fingers of the hand were spread like a fan. The air faintly whistled through them with each stroke of Dundeed's wrist.

How was Dundeed playing with me, I wondered.

Turning toward Doyle to see what message might be scrawled across his watchful face, I saw that he had vanished. And indeed the hand with which Dundeed had so daringly seized the moment could only have done so by releasing Doyle, by putting him off the leash. I seemed to hear it lashing the floor after a clatter of diminishing footsteps. Through a back door.

Only the two of us then, and a ghostly third hovering between. How like we are now. We three here.

I turned in reply to the ghostly touch upon my shoulder, only to face Dundeed's laughter. The black wraith of the mummified arm, he now so gingerly brandished above his head, was missing a finger. Like a porcelain-shelled beetle, it clung to my shoulder. The coarse grain of mummified tissue grabs as tenaciously as the tarsus claw of the beetle leg. Two finger joints, as segmented as mandible and thorax. Deft specimen collector that I am, I palmed it in a motion more winged than the most predatory beak.

Dundeed made no move. He merely snorted a last clot of mucoid laughter into the back of his throat and hastily redrew the wan smile upon his lips. He winked. The light in his eye shot towards me, as if it were a marble, with the snap of a sharpshooter's thumb behind it.

I opened my hand. I pushed the tip of my finger against the dry knuckle. It was wet. A licorice smear. You'd be thinking of the policeman's ink blotter, wouldn't you? Then sprout your policeman's antennae, the bug-eyed ommatidia of your detective insight, and see what I have been telling you. He is an old man, but he is a killer. So now you know: truth was the first casualty of that malice. And now the crime is yours to confront as steadily as I stood before it that day.

Didn't Dundeed then drop what I now knew to be the exotically manicured arm to the floor, as if it were nothing more than a bone for a dog—yes, the unleashed dog was long gone—in order to unsheathe his rapier reach, fastening his fist upon my collar with force enough to pop a button, to shred a seam, for me to feel the impress of my Adam's apple upon my vocal chords? In the tiniest bones of my ears I registered a noise like the pounding of a tiny mallet upon the strings of a hand-sized glass piano.

My breath stood up stiffly in the narrow constriction of my throat, like an audience at applause.

All the while the warm wave action of his belly threatened to bounce me off my feet. He stood that close. No doubt the flabbiness of the ocean is capable of dealing the severest smacks.

No. He didn't strike me, though Dundeed's other hand, as large as a small frying pan, twitched against his tumescent flank. He only said that he trusted me.

Again, he sliced across the glaucous fish eye with a heavy lid. Wink of an eye. Resuscitation of the smile on his thin lips with a few short, coughing breaths. He stepped back with the frying pan hand resting on his paunch. And then he very grandiosely bowed.

As he righted himself, the hand swung loosely out from the hinge of his body, like the violently tugged end of a velvet bellpull, making a florid gesture toward the door that I had barged through only minutes—beaded now like perspiration upon my consciousness—before.

I felt like someone from whom a precious gift has been taken away, barely moments before the wrapping is completely off the box. Didn't I now know something that he wished me to keep as a secret, without uttering it even to myself, because the words weren't mine to use? But hadn't I known it already? And didn't I know that he didn't?

Remember?

x x x x x

FIELD INVENTORY: (December, 1999) Specimen #26, Crate #6

Hermaphrodite. Head and body. Male genitalia likewise separated from the trunk. The specimen survives in an extraordinary state of preservation. 25 centimeters fall of ochre-dyed hair intact upon skull. One vertebrae exposed below the collar of skin. Facial features almost flushed with the finesse of skin tone. Skin pores closed by lapidary humidification. Lips, nostrils, eyebrows, lashes, tear ducts, all impeccably etched.

Only the eyes have been savaged. Residue of charcoal and pine splinters scars the cavities. The torso and lower body are fully extended, but warped, by some buoyancy that has left the spine arched, the arms and legs dangling, as if the whole body were still afloat upon an undulant depth.

Then there is the torment to consider. The scrotal sac, pierced by a dozen wooden pins. They are all short enough to be concealed—except for the barely detectable perforations—within. Impossible to explain how they are so finely milled.

An atrocious act.

Women of science, because we are more finely attuned to such suffering, will be its most human custodians. Differences of anatomy notwithstanding. I only ask for the recognition that we have earned. Why shouldn't our compassion be a calculable asset of our knowing?

We are the hermaphrodites of our profession. If we probe the black earth with our long spades, should we not suckle its tarry children? And if we cuddle them a touch too close to the breast, who, after all, would wish to punish us for that? I ask you.

Who do I ask?

x x x x x

I understand his distasteful accusation. It is only my memory, not my cerebrum, that ails, that is if you honor the doctor's diagnosis. And haven't I heard the charge before, hurled by less jealously enflamed competitors? Shall I say the word myself? For authenticity's sake? Do you want to hear it from my lips?

"Forgery."

Ah, but the act of forgery comes most naturally to the emotions. So perhaps our Taste does know whereof he speaks.

I have it in my book. My book remembers.

He thinks she loves him back. He says he has that feeling, as reliably as a good digestion. Rubbing his belly, he means to mock me? He is taunting me even before I have tendered him the blessing he so painfully solicits?

But I don't have to go by his words alone. I have seen Roscoe Taste and Cinnabar McDermond as a couple. I have seen him proffering her galoshes at the door, trussing her in furs and oilcloths before the door is opened to the knocking wind. He has basked in the gleam of the teeth that he mistook for her smile. Because I have watched her soak up his eyes until barely the pupils remained, like stray seeds of a ravished fruit, and I have seen myself how little he discerned the forger's art in the creamy flesh tones of that woman's affection. I saw him hold her cheek, fastidious where to mount his lips—too much like a dog marking the ground I must say—before he deposited his tenderness upon the reef of the cheekbone. An ungainly perch. You would have noticed that her eyes never closed, her thin lips molted the gesture of any reciprocal feeling. Her smile was a desiccated skin that would have blown away under the advance of his most intimate breathing, the gentlest brush of his mustache.

Once he brought her on his arm, to an evening convocation of the National Archeological Society, where I would speak. "Curations of the Living Dead" was the amusing party mask with which I beribboned my topic: Preservation of Tissue Integument Under Stresses of Specimen Exhibition.

Cinna's pearl shoulders shone radiantly above an onyx décolletage. Then this Taste had his arm draped around her. His hand appeared reddened like a garish broach, pinned directly upon the flesh, in the lee of the right shoulder, a few archly calibrated centimeters beyond the furthest velvet reach of the gown upon her breast.

I looked out from the podium that night with a full command of the room. My voice was strong and clear.

But I spoke with my eyes that night, watching, through the telescopic probings of my words the two members of my audience for whom I reserved my most acute focus. I spoke of tegumental integrity and the paradoxical porosity of cell walls, whereby the very organism that retains its form is replaced by its mineral surround and is thereafter understood to be no place and everywhere, a bit like the eye which loses its sense of motor coordination in the fine grain of its focus on a detail so miniscule the muscle begins to grind upon itself, as if it were being pierced by a pin.

That night my eye was a bubble about to burst. Where I could spy the indecent couple in the back of the low-beamed meeting room, beneath the flickering lattice shadow of a palm frond, incessantly rustled by rude traffic up and down the aisle, they sat now under the caress of Cinna's hand. The hand, braceletted and pale, might have been an albino ferret on a leash, adhering to the dark material of Taste's suit with clawed agility. A roving snout. Nipping a silver button, nosing the inner chartreuse lining of the breast pocket and tentatively delving into the shadowy lap where it seemed to pounce upon a burrow. Would it emerge with the wildly spinning legs and whirring tail of a struggling mouse body, agitating the air like a pinwheel in its maw? Hers was not the affectionate hand.

No, the affectionate hand belonged to Roscoe Taste that night; however, much the silkiness of its seduction was little more than an instinctual slither around her shoulders. The hand was his. But the eye was mine. Eye to eye.

The eye is the prize sense, after all. Cinna never took hers off me. Leaning at my podium, the swimmer breasting the long course of water ahead of him, I was, for the duration of my lecture, invisibly propped upon the green dilated depth of Cinna's concentrating pupil. Buoyed by the yellow-feathered scintillations of such unblinking eyewash, was I not walking on water?

That was how I understood the forgery she was perpetrating against a man who was clearly possessed of no discerning taste whatsoever.

There they were, when all my words were spent. After the effervescence of the question and answer period had brought the audience to their feet, applauding, I saw Taste and Cinna clinking champagne glasses above the honey-basted head of a suckling pig, struck wide-eyed, and crowning one end of the buffet table, where the guests had begun to gather for the digestion of my ideas.

The two of them. Talking. Face to face.

But, when I entered the room, Cinna was still watching me. She looked past him, even as she seemed to pass her words like salubrious tidbits from her mouth to his, so closely did she bow her head to him.

She even swept her eyes, with the smoothness of a petting hand, over his brow in a convincing gesture of endearment that, to the more discerning eye, was the playful ruse of losing me on one side of his head and finding me on the other, as I crossed the floor. Her gaze swiveled on her neck like the painter's avid brushstroke, filling in an area of background sea or sky with a metronomic twisting of the wrist, no doubt bringing the central figure more contrastively into the foreground. I felt myself coming forward.

I didn't have to move.

She put her hand so softly to his cheek that he let its caress turn his head—far enough for her to give me her most open-faced communication over his shoulder. She formed the words wordlessly on lips, so protuberant with pantomime, that the contorted silence might have snagged her tongue on a paroxysm of involuntary speech. The darkness that liquefied within the circumference of those lips I knew was nothing less than what stirred her loins as she pressed herself more intimately against Taste's shivering frame and made him—how oblivious to the forger's genius stroke!—a resonant membrane between us. Hymenal? Virginal? How would this deflowering be consummated?

Anyone watching in this room, already bustling with portly bodies gravitating towards the buffet, gathering density, bumping against one another in the faintly toasted air that was also expanding, stoked by the peated flame—a fireplace, the height of the man strong enough to pile its massive field stones one upon the other, poured light like hot oil upon the roiling throng—would have been blind to what I saw. So bloated with their own physicality. The buffet guests would have been oblivious to any sensations not already their own. Like Taste himself, I had no doubt.

So, in a most curious way, in that moment of crossed gazes, Cinna and I were like unchaperoned lovers alone for the first time. We were alone in our attunement to the artfulness of her dissimulating fingers invisibly unhooking the middle buttons of Taste's shirt, pulling gently upon the panting tongue of his opened belt—all in the blind light of the public eye!—rouging the back of his neck, and so, no doubt, his cheeks as well, with the heat of her inner thigh slowly rising upon the back of his leg. Pointing with the toe that had lifted the elegantly tapering leg high enough to make the hem of her gown slide frothily to the hip, she had been showing me that the pressure of this most labile joint of her body against the fulcrum of his groin was the lever that had opened her mouth to me, in silent but unmistakable candor. Over his shoulder the feline moan that had surely heated the inner coils of this Taste's violet ear had mouthed to me the words "I love you."

Hadn't her daring eyes been opened with the same imploring dilation as the quavering mouth? Did they not behold the very "you" that her lips still held as firmly as the last note of an aria, sustained with such inexhaustible breath that it will be undistinguishable from the silence that lingers in the empty chamber when no one is listening?

So the false touch, by which Cinna had quickened the limbs of this man of no discerning taste, had made true lovers of us after all.

The forgery of love has a diabolical provenance, to be sure. But what a prize it makes of the genuine article! And the genuine article was mine, not his. The discerning eye takes a rightful pride in knowing that the real thing may only be authenticated in the here and now, where the sultry pleasures, because they are not answerable to any other moment in time, are indisputable.

The forgery always harkens toward a time past. The fooled lover is the one who has to remember what he looked like to possess the feeling, if he wishes to reprise it in the arms of another. That's Taste's dilemma. The fooled lover never ceases to need to be fooled again. But because he depends on likenesses, he will never mollify his doubt that who he is, in the here and now, is different beyond recognition.

× × × × ×

I'll tell you what can't be falsified—death. My mother's death. Who else would they call to identify the body? I had to go home.

I had to descend into what can only be described as a sewer. The rungs of the rubberized rope ladder—they were already fouled with gritty boot-scrapings of the metal-capped team of rescuers milling above and below—grew slicker with the wriggling dampness of my descent.

But the pecking stench against which the white-faced rescuers were trying to defend themselves, with handkerchiefs and goggle-eyed face masks designed to protect against the sting of smoke and flame, was my homing scent. Even if it flexed a knuckle of disgust in the pit of my stomach, it always quickened my pulse. And unlike the fire brigadiers, so perspiringly attired for the wrong disaster, in metal-soled boots and rubber greatcoats—they therefore could not have fathomed what manner of calamity awaited them at the bottom of such a sulphurous, but positively clammy pit—I knew what to expect.

A deep pit indeed. At bottom, a kind of dead sea, also deep, but waterless. It never surged. Yet it continuously bubbled to expel gases brewed from the indigestible refuse of freshly butchered chickens. The pit was filled, with tidal regularity, by the viscous conveyer belts that crisscrossed the looming hangar space of the small processing plant floor. All pretensions to sheep herding aside, this was our family's real livelihood. Chickens. The pit was a midden of spongy lungs and bilious gall bladders, gizzards calcified with the blind ingestion of oyster shells, pebbles, metal beads, buttons, clods of earth. And then there were the aghast beaks and shrieking eyes, a confetti of feathers, and of course eggs. Eggs without shells. Sometimes a string of three or four would be released on the stroke of the gutting blade, each buoyant and elastic to the touch as a racing pulse. They would bob on the surface until blackened with the coagulation of the capillary blood that breathes through them.

All of this was knowable, if one could see into the stagnant abyss, if one had eyes with shovel handles to pry beneath the heavy shadows sedimented there by the thirty-foot rise of corrugated aluminum walls, standing at right angles to the pit. So, one needed the incandescence of four mercury vapor flood lights trained upon the bottom of the pit, to alchemize the brute matter of unventilated stench into the weightless lucidity that would reveal the victim floating face down, her skirts inflated about her like a child's water wings—two lobes of trapped air—while her head and arms were lost beneath the surface as if she were a hacked torso. Despite the etching intensity of illumination that rendered the body unmistakable from a dry perch above, the impatient rescuers, issuing smoky commands from behind the turreted housings of the floodlights, insisted that the son descend fifteen rungs of the ladder, immersing one leg to the thigh in order to verify the face. They refused to raise the victim before he recognized her. Did they imagine that somehow she had become the creature of where she had fallen? Excuse enough to abandon her where she had fallen?

But of course she had not fallen. She had jumped.

And I have already shown you her face. I wager you could

have recognized her yourself. Green eyes, haloed with hammered gold. No, Cinna was not her name. But the resemblance! Haven't I told you, you can go by the resemblance?

The greasy pole the rescuers had thrust upon me for righting the body bore a curlicued hook at its end, barbed on the inside, so that it might be used as a lever as well as a blade. But at the swaying bottom of the ladder the ungainly extension of it swung beyond my control to pierce a shoulder. I felt the heartthrob of a fish on the line, which torqued the reflexes in my wrist enough to accomplish the feat of overturning the body. But then I could not see straight enough to keep to my path.

Piercing the flesh, seeing the face, seemingly all in one motion, twirled me off my already unsteady footing into a fetid gyre. I was flailing. The temptation to execute swimming strokes recoiled from the sensation of thickly granulated substance, of loamish buoyancy, vile, slithering scrapings against my ankles and shins, nipping my toes, curding under my armpits, so fouling the membrane of my sinuses with the fungal yeasting of sugary spores, that I was sure I tasted it. I might have swallowed my own nose though my lips were fiercely and belligerently sealed.

Now the rescuers could no longer avoid their official duty. Because, in my frantic efforts to raise my mouth and nose and eyes above the gurgling surface—made more tempestuous by the flailing of my arms—I came face to face with my mother's ultimate grimace. The green eyes open, but as rigidly flat and metallic as fish scales, the mouth crookedly aghast at its own fate and dribbling the contents of the sewer into which she had hurled her anger. Such anger had so long besieged her body, she might very well have imagined this to be her only recourse for prying the gnarled talons loose from her soul.

Thus was I doubly in need of a helping hand.

And waiting for the rope to be coiled and tossed a second time from a middle rung of the ladder, now steadied by two earnestly crouching brigadesmen at the top of the shaft—shouting in frenetically raucous tones for me to calm myself—I was forced to gag upon the question that bobbed between my mother and myself like the most loathsome flotsam imaginable in such a place.

Had she abandoned me at last, as she had sworn never to do? Was this dark and dank midden of deliquescent chicken parts my orphanage? Was I being childish to think that all my childhood fears of being left behind—in the urinal of a train station, at the gate of the empty schoolyard, in the parked car, even astride the rearing carousel stallion whose dizzying gallop blurred my view of the responsible parent watching, from behind the confetti colored ropes, waiting to take me home—were realized here?

It was not true.

Here is my proof. I had already confided Cinna's pregnancy. I had told mother our secret. I had imparted the seed in her ear.

And when I whispered my news into her cupped ear, I had seen in the wetness of my mother's green eye something like the concentric circles that form when a fish nibbles the yet unbroken surface of an algae-skinned pond.

Was it succor enough for my mother to know that without her, now and forever more, I would never be left alone?

Had the tiny seed of my future happiness sprouted the fully leafed thought that so manifestly bloated this lifeless body? I suspect that it had lain dormant in her since the first blow of my father's open hand had turned her cheek, like the proverbial spade against the proverbial rock. Didn't she now imagine that at long last she was no longer sole protectoress of the child whose rickety limbs, strung together by his fears, made for a ceaselessly trembling frame? Didn't she know that my worst fear in childhood was finding her eyes like empty saucers of milk staring up at me from the yellow trough in the pillow where she'd gently laid the swollen jaw, the abraded ear, the feverish knot on the back of the head, to heal? Knowing all this—when I imparted the secret of Cinna's propitious fertility—didn't she feel as if the most livid muscle had loosened in the pit of her stomach, and sigh?

And if this is the truth, wouldn't Cinna's child be mine by a chain of reasons that—link by iron link—should be strong enough to garrote an elephant? The green eye is my witness, is it not?

A mother does not abandon her only child before he is provided for by nature. She is nature's local self and family representative. Cinna's green eye shimmers. I'm sure in your recollection that I have always been a lover of nature, and that our first encounter—Cinna's and mine—was a tribute to natural resemblance. Her avid eye licking the glossy surfaces of my photograph album dry was proof of that, I should think.

So I ask you to find enough skepticism in your heart that when you hear the slanderous tongue of this Emeritus gloryhound lapping at the door of your credulity with his slurping insinuations, his solicitous words, beaded with honeyed milkdroplets of empathy, you might consider the possibility of emotional forgery.

Haven't I said it forcefully enough yet? Dundeed is not whom he appears to be.

Not the self-inflictedly pained truth-teller who bleeds for his victim's wounds, mourns the necessity of such tormented honesty, as he would try to convince you is his alone. He would even attend the funerals of the hopes he's murdered, solemnized in suffocating black crepe. Wouldn't he just?

No, he's a right shite and all. A corrosive quim-stream of fish bile. A vain cum smear of envy. A shite-hawk wanker. Sodding bog pumper. Withering goat ballocks. A teetering beaker of stale piss, his every word scintillating with the golden fetor of his own shame, his pent up agonies, the scalding iron of guilt that pinks in the livid eye of his rectum.

Winking bastard.

x x x x x

You can't expect me to answer such vulgarity. But I have my book. My book remembers the oaths I've borne.

Cinna begged for marriage, and I swore to her wish. So simple. It was on a day flooded with sunlight…

No! It wasn't a rare day of sun as I had first remembered. The fog was invasive. A lining of fur in the eyes and nose, sloe wax in the ears. A woolen tongue in the mouth. Like something already prevalent to the sense that discerns it. Impossible to escape. At the bottom of an eight-foot trench the air is already too deep for easy breathing.

No, it was not the trench. I had only thought so. Please remember.

No. It was the furthest spit of unpeated ground extending into the quashy deeps that ringed the find site. The only solid ground. In the days of the reed communities, standing where we were then, one would have stared across an eddying expanse of green water. From a flat bottomed boat, little more than a mat of reeds athwart a frame of loosely notched logs, it would have looked as though the canopy of a dense forest undulated in a somnolent lemon-tinted breeze below the surface. We think they were not good swimmers.

I remember. I do remember. Cinna held my hand against the narrow slope. A big man is always a liability on inclining ground. But her grip only tightened as we balanced more precariously on the spiny relief of the land's end.

No! No! No! None of it. None of it at all.

I do remember. I remember it differently. It was the night the dogs were mysteriously loosed into a wind that took their baying with it, up the slopes of the nearby hills. Cinna awoke to the silence in the crook of my arm. Her eyes drained of sleep were mostly white as she shook me alive.

The fog was as white against the black hour. The electric lines that powered the floodlights in four corners of the find site had been cut, as cleanly as the chains that were bolted to the dog's collars. The ribbons of pathway that threaded between the deep trenches were even more like tightropes to the blind footstep.

For a man as large as myself, the feat of crossing that pitted field would have been unimaginable without Cinna's intrepid grip. Looking down without fear of losing the balance that was not my own, I could see a white froth of fog faintly illuminating our footsteps, as though we were splashing through shallow water.

Surefooted as she was, Cinna knew where we were going. In our haste, we had overlooked the battery belt that otherwise powered the torch, now a useless weight in my free hand. When I proposed going back, she boasted her eyes would be as bright.

And she immediately proved the phosphorescence of her boast by showing me—her arms strapped around my chest, holding the weight of me against a trough of empty air—where we stood. At the sheer edge of the trench I felt its darker humidity breathe upon my lower body like a wet stain spreading on a trouser leg. Here, only the day before, we had made a discovery that was already roaring news in the village, though the specimens weren't yet out of the ground.

So we had thought.

Without descending to the sense of touch we both knew, with palpitating certainty, that what we treasured had been ravished from its intaglio in the peated floor of the trench.

The "Bridal Couple" we had already christened them. That was what the papers had already proclaimed.

"Long awaited additions to the repertory of our bog playlets and footlight favorites to boot..." Roscoe Taste had sneered at the banner headline in the local GAZETTE.

But the discovery was nothing of the stock in trade, which is why we had been uncharacteristically patient to excavate. We hesitated, lest our full comprehension of the ecstatic entanglement of those still simmering limbs should elude us as ephemerally as the last indrawn breaths of the victims themselves.

The specimens in the bog are above all the preservatives of time. Obviously. But perhaps we oversimplify by treating them like medicinal condiments in the bell jar of our quaintly apothecary notions of the past.

The light which reveals them, gleaming first from the beveled edges of spade and trowel, is the mirror glass through which we see them in the here and now that was only theirs.

Their moment is alive, if they are not. That is what we respected in our reticence to extract the specimens willy-nilly from their natural matrix.

The couple had lain, as if still falling through air upon a collapsing bed, borne downward by their pelvic centers of gravity, arms and legs aloft of the torsos. The female's hair crowned with a wreathe of brambles was a flow of lush incarnadine tresses, slipped from the skullcap to nestle against a black cheek. The pelt itself was such a marvel of preservation. That alone would have guaranteed our illustrious mention in a specialized volume of one of the archeological digests—a volume devoted to hair. But Cinna and I looked for our reward in the evidence of a ritual that had all the trappings—simultaneously—of a wedding and an execution.

The "Bride's" girdle, of a coarse tabby weave, but striped with a blue pigment and stiffened with painted fish vertebrae, was the obvious mate to the male's wreathe of roses. Of course we can only imagine what flower was twined around the worsted flaxen sash that hung to his navel. All of this, and especially the tiny iron ring clenched between his teeth and embittered lips, rang the bells of our recognition of something nuptial. And hadn't there been a bouquet in her right hand, held as it was in such a loosely bunched fist? They were otherwise both naked.

The impassioned contents of the bride's other hand were less speculatively grasped. Her grublike fingers, inarticulable from the dun-colored flap of crusted skin that almost seemed to be threaded through them, were, upon closer inspection, knotted around the groom's unmistakable sex, the time-deflated remnant of which belied the more virile purchase that must have held the bride so assiduously to her moment. Even in midair, flung beyond the lip of solid turf, catapulted from the dancing shoulders of the exuberant celebrants—merrymakers who in their jubilant frenzy were perhaps even sobbingly incapable of telling their true loves from their true hatreds—the bridal couple flew in tandem to their enduring demise.

And the smiles. The smiles on their faces are the final conundrum of their fate. Did they believe they were being carried, in the goat-faced spirit of some primitive chivaree, to the carnival molestations of the marriage bed? Or did they know the jubilant shoulders upon which they rode were the cages of their capture? Their smiles were little more than crusted ripples in drying mud.

Their smiles! But Cinna and I knew their smiles would have rattled the glass case in which they would have been famously exhibited, as violently, as if the specimens within were struggling to escape. The shaken museum-goer would have wondered: did those who hurled the couple hold them high for some curious ritual of ebullient worship, or only for a better trajectory into the mire?

Such confusion between air and earth is so apt a coda for the enigmatic disappearance of the specimens themselves. For gone they were.

The darkly foreseen emptiness of the trench, when it was finally illumined by the repowered floodlights an hour before dawn, yawned more vacuously with the higher resolution of our scrutiny. I believe it was the bare imprint of two backbones curled in the bottom of the trench, like freshly shed snake skins, that charmed the sinuous words from Cinna's lips: "Marry me then." She held the dawning sun in her eyes like shimmering coins to pay her passage to that beyond. I said "yes," courteous ferryman that I am.

What a double misfortune (Is it nevertheless a sign, that everything we know we know in couples?) that nothing in my account of these events can be confirmed? For the physical evidence goes missing still. What kind of criminal mind denies us the truth we know? What kind of criminal mind possesses the necessary skills? Neither the notorious international black market in mummies, nor the most disreputable museums—with whom the police maintain dutifully unsavory relations, the better to inveigle their cooperation—have divulged a trace of the vanished specimens. Because what can be made to disappear can never be authenticated, the crime is curiously identical to the forger's deceit.

But I make no accusations.

x x x x x

I never did propose marriage. Wouldn't you think the child was bond enough between us? Cinna and I.

I will admit that Cinna's body seemed, even weeks after the announcement, untouched by any virulent seed of conception. Not so much as an angry rash had yet raised the vellum surface of her eerily pacific belly when I finally offered to show her something that I imagined *she* would be as keen to see.

A jaunt to the nearby village required a bicycle. Cinna, almost weightless by contrast with my curious hopes for her belly, sat sidesaddle upon the yellow bar that rattled my striving groin with each rickety cranking of the pedals.

In that bogscape there are no trees to calibrate the speed or distance. Only a drear impasto, the color of dead leaves, caked upon the panoramic expanse. It gives the appearance of an abandoned canvas, the artist turned sullenly from the easel with clotted fingertips. To pass the time otherwise I suppose, there was a kind of song in Cinna's throat, a low clicking. I heard it against my rhythmic pumping of the pedals. My own ear rising to and falling from proximity to her white voice, with each stroke of our progress down the road, was a metronome to the sound that was, at that point, barely distinguishable from the slipping of the bicycle chain against the cogs of the drive wheel. Had I sliced her open at that moment would I have revealed the inner workings of the metal automaton, all noisy gears and a shower of electrical sparks? Her spine was stiff as a rod before me. I might have beat myself onward with it.

I didn't ask her the name or the meaning of the song, in the same way I didn't ask her to marry me.

I only wanted her to follow me around the stone buttress where I had left the bicycle dripping with my perspiration, or, yes, more likely, the dew that hangs on in that part of the country until nigh noon. Here was a small cobbled street, absolutely deserted. Churchless, shopless. Only five or six grim-faced stone cottages staring at each other across the emerald cobbles, choked with moss. Casementless windows, stove in doors that had once been brightly painted blue or white and a quartet of shattered gas lamps, mourned the silence of the street.

Of course no one lived in the village, nor had they since the famine of a hundred and twenty years past.

I say past. But it is nothing to an archeologist, a hundred years. We are still too present to it. Of course he'll tell you different, the old man, the unfamished fuck.

Cinna appeared unexpectedly in front of me, where I turned from searching behind me for her. She thrust her hand at me as if she were leading the way. Unusually carefree she seemed. She must have imagined that being fecklessly open to the emptiness of the abandoned stones would suffice for filling the expanse of the afternoon with whatever idle pleasures I had put in store for us.

Where then was the picnic lunch that should have fettered my progress up the slope behind her? Where the straw-colored wicker basket laden with tinned meats and bottled fruits, the bulky flagon of wine that wants chilling in the burbling brook, the scratchy blanket that wants spreading over a grassy hillock? No rattling delicacies. No brook. No grass. Only the dead silence of the street, washed in the gray light of an afternoon that anyone could already see would be indistinguishable from the dawn that was, and the dusk to come.

But once forced to stand at the top of a gloomy crypt of cellar steps, Cinna's face gave shape to a more ravenous appetite than sandwiches and candied condiments would have satisfied. I watched her in profile descend the first steps. I saw the scientist awaken, shake off the slackness of the features with which she had countenanced an idle day like loose bed sheets. I saw her lick her lips, tasting the spore that gives the humid air its special tang if you are a born digger.

No doubt Cinna could see that the door had been bolted. But now the clean bite that left the deadbolt in two pieces revealed the sheen of its new steel under the flat black finish. Cinna's hand pushed brusquely past my meticulously contrived aura of mystery, as unfazed as a person stepping heedlessly through a curtain of ectoplasm.

Her unexpected haste caused us to come too quickly to the scene of recognition I had so patiently set myself. Cinna had even reckoned upon the electric light switch, grafted to the corroded plaster of the ancient wall where only candlelight would ever have shone its unpainted, pitted surface to the shaky hand that needed to lean upon it, should the shock of what the small room contained be so great. I had so thought it would be.

As I rushed up behind her, poised to put my hands on her shoulders, to support her in the watery-kneed moment of amazement that otherwise might have left her puddled on the dirt floor, she turned to me with a white finger stiffening at her lips. Her eyes were not bulging with what she had seen. The green was not made more prominent by the dilation of their credulity.

Had she even seen it?

There were three pallets raised on rickety sawhorses. Two human bodies, one canine. Two steps into the room and one sniffed a forest, until one realized the sensation of slippery depths underfoot was only shallow drifts of sawdust carpeting the floor. In one corner of the room the store of softly bulging gunny sacks resembled a hiving litter of puppies nuzzling for a single teat. And then there was the sewing apparatus that stood angrily in its black cast-iron frame against the far wall, clawed and tangled in a coarse hempen thread, as if it had gone mad in some final frenzy of its operation.

It was a workroom, of course. Even a laboratory, if one were to indulge a metaphor.

"Now do you see?" I trammeled the admonition of Cinna's finger in an exasperated shout. "It is what we both suspected, a forger's atelier, a property room fit for a troupe of local theatricals, a mingy costuming loft where you can be bearded and masked for two pence. Call it what you wish. We're all falsified now!"

"This is Doyle. Are you blind?" Cinna's finger made a swordsman's zigzagging flourish before my eyes.

"Are you mad?"

"This is Doyle. I could see it at once."

"But Doyle *is* Dundeed, his reasonable facsimile in any case, his cousin creature, such peas, such a pod."

Cinna sucked at her breath, as if resisting the temptation to swallow. She cast a harried, birdlike glance over her shoulder, returned to my inquisitorial stare, suppressed a sneeze with a hideously muscular squint and an almost wooly furrowing of her brow.

"You see things always by their likenesses. That's your problem," she hissed, almost indistinguishably from the sneeze. "Dundeed is different. It is Doyle's museum. Only the museum profits Doyle in a way that crime would benefit. It's Doyle. Only Doyle."

Did she push me back, push past me, her knuckles knocking belligerently against the thinness of my breastbone? She was gone in any event, as if she had never been present. I was alone, facing the three fraudulent specimens in their mortuary reposes. And I had no notion of what materials—natural or manmade—the most epidermal layer of these artful physiques was mocking by its uncanny resemblance to peated preservation. Aping the grizzled brownness, the tobacco leaf texture that gives pause to the man with the shovel—since he stands upon ground of the same composition—they looked somehow more primitive for all the evidence of their recent manufacture.

Would touch tell differently, I wondered? It did not. My fingertip tarnished with the same dry talc that made a thin paste in the lavatory wash basin at the end of the workday.

The bicycle was gone of course when, famished myself, I turned my back on all that had been abandoned upon these moss and lichen-covered stones decades before because they gave no sustenance to anything human. By the time I reached the stone corner where I had leaned the rusty pedaled contraption, its being gone was the perfect match for my breathlessness.

On the road below me I spied Cinna's back, laboring above the hard dark foot pedals, rising and falling in what could easily have been mistaken for the sultry rhythm of sexual ardor, her head bobbling ecstatically between her shoulder blades. My feet were sluggish, even in descent. My eye wearily traversed the distance those feet would have to take me now.

When I arrived at the perimeter of the find site, Cinna was waiting in the spindly shadow of the flagstaff, pensive under the rude flutter of the university insignia. Something about her had changed. Not the manner of her dress—always the same black patent boots, khaki jodhpurs, and epauletted field shirt. But the measure of the material was larger by at least two sizes and it hung like a picture of dishevelment from her otherwise swank frame.

I noticed the shirttail loose in the breeze, which I had never seen untucked. That was what she wanted to show me with the coyly miniaturized gesture of one crooked finger tugging at me from the center of her face, where her cocked wrist barely obscured the smile baiting the hook.

Having walked this far, the remaining steps were as easeful as removing my boots for a waiting pan of hot suds. Cinna took me by the hand, and seeming to know where I wished to put it myself, drew the sensitive fingers under the loose shirttail, to the scintillating braille text of her belly. Was it the solemn deliberation with which she moved my hand, or the irrepressibility of my desire to go there, that persuaded my sense of touch to note a perceptible tumescence around the navel, a subtle bulking of the taut musculature that was otherwise the bracing trampoline of our fiercest sexual play?

She said nothing, but only began again—in the most constricted spaces of her throat—to force the notes of the song that had seemed to rattle the hollow tubes of the bicycle much earlier in the day. And so the lumbering ache in my calves and thigh muscles returned with the fruitless rhythm of the bicycle pedals, rising and plunging like the resolute prow of a ship. I feared I was on the proverbial journey that never ends and let the fear wash over me, knowing in the most desiccated cranny of my nature, that I would never be dry again.

x x x x x

FIELD INVENTORY: (February 2000) Specimen #34, Crate #13

Male: 2 meters, 31 centimeters in length. Naked except for a worsted cape—berry dyed—and one worsted legging adhering to the right leg by some cellular chemistry that has rendered the epidermis inextricable from the woolen weave. A girth of 139 centimeters. Extraordinary even for a human specimen of this scale!

The heft of the limbs—and not least the crowning belly—has posed a challenge to the preservative elements, and so a conundrum to our bog expertise, tutored as it is by dampness and the exchange of gases whispering the permeability of all membranous matter, animal and vegetable alike. By our most professional reckoning, only the more superficial dermal layers are permeable enough to perpetuate the definition of cell structure.

Then do the most internal vaults of a body so big as this one paradoxically become chambers of decay, inner sinks of deliquescence, underground sewers? Or, are they like the geodes of the geologist's severe alembic, precincts of perfect crystallization, where every berry and leaf of the intestinal flora is shiveringly intact? Could it be that the crust of the preserved epidermis becomes even more preservative of what it conceals, like the mummy case to which the flesh and blood likenesses of the figurines within are beholden? And which of us "mummy men"—for all the brotherhood implied, I speak for women of science after all—which of us has not imagined an undiscovered link between the dank bottoms of this overly humidified plain and the blazing peaks of the pyramids, ashimmer on the desert's ever-liquefying horizon?

And if it is true—that size is preservative—then this specimen of the male belly, so magnified by the symptom of its gigantism, augurs well for the dilated scrutiny of the scientific eye unaided by lenses and the other cumbersome prosthetics of discovery. Only the indispensable knife and the naked eye, glinting at its focal point, are needed: one sharpness whetting the steely edge of the other.

I must think of the specimen belly as an archeological treasure chest, the cornucopia of its digestions overflowing the sectioned cavity with lapidary evidence of everything he has eaten and the world he has eaten from. The grit in the oat cake, the fly in the undigested teardrop of honey, the segmented apple core (three bites?), the nut of the crankberry, the fine combed hair of wild grasses—but how could these have filled him up?—will give us purchase on the natural tableau, against which his existence can be seen more vividly by our museum patrons. Noses to the glass, fingernails drumming, their heads will swoon in dioramic space.

From the contents of the stomach, the immortal sedimentia, the slivered sections of the impeccable gut, we will glean pigments to paint the landscape that was dwarfed by, and may even have seemed to quake under, the staggering shadow of this gigantic physique.

We will stand him up, if the available devices make it possible to hide the wires. He may even cast his shadow on the glass. Anyone peering through will know that the authenticity of the landscape is the inventory of everything he has eaten, extrapolated to the sense of sight. A printed card will say so: SEE THE BERRY BUSH, A HEATHERLIKE UNDERGROWTH, A STUNTED APPLE TREE, A HIVE GLOWING FROM WITHIN A ROCK CREVICE, A STAND OF TALL GRASSES THAT REACH BARELY TO HIS CALF.

Surely there is such a connection between one sense and another—the eye and the tongue—in this case a reverse osmosis. What was ingested, and flowed with the tidal blood through the walls of the body, bleeds back and becomes a vision of itself again.

Women of science have such a rapport with the human belly, the total permeability of the body, that they can make this assertion. I'm not referring to the time-honored woes of childbirth and penetration as our entitlement to say such things. Mine is not a statement of political passion. Not a sentimental ointment to be rubbed into the wounds of some brutalized history.

I know something more particular.

The belly of a man, more than twice the size of a typical modern specimen—and especially because the circumstances of the preservation are unique with respect to the innermost organs—reminds us that when they are buried, the bodies are conveyances of the very earth that hugs them close.

In the diorama we must see—make a note to the technician—that there is an unbreakable bond between the body and its places. It is the flow of time of course, which this massive stomach encrypts. My puns are so deep, they want an excavation of their own. But let us instead envision the curvature of the back wall of the diorama. What vista can be painted there to take in all that we may have discovered from our probing of the knowledgeable gut? What color of the sky is imparted by the resinous curd of undigested grape?

But of course, the cranial deformity makes me wonder if our specimen himself knew anything at all about the light, or even mucous gray swirl of dampness in which he flourished. The eyes are both punched deeply beneath the overhanging brow. This was not a violence worked upon him by human hands. A more gigantic power must have pushed furious thumbs into the dough of this face to make these eyes appear so blind. And the hairless bud of chin, that might have dripped from the tip of the beaky nose, makes a mockery of the mouth that droops imploringly above it. Was there mandible bone enough even to chew what passed between those lips? Was the humped shoulder a painful counterweight to the belly that made even walking upright a perversity of nature? Could there be a more punishing hand than the one that touched this hapless creation alive?

Time to speculate later. I must fly, my diary. But I have so much more to share. Wait for me! Wait!

You ask again how I knew she loved me. And haven't I already tested your disbelief in me, even to the point of my deepest shame? I have admitted that I am an old man pilloried by fat, a sagging girdle of wrinkled flesh, a sink of decay, a veritable sewer to the vital juices that effervesced my youthful *esprit*. And haven't I welcomed this degradation as proof of my fundamental honesty—if that isn't too much dignity to accord myself—at this extremity of your interrogation?

How did I know she loved me?

Step up for your answer. Come. Stand closer again. I need to whisper. I need to feel the proximity of your breathing and maybe even the lean of you—a fat man's indulgence, I beg it—since it will bring her nearer to mind. She leaned on me. Isn't that what I'm saying? And you will insist upon my remembering.

Here and now I can remind you that she loved me not for my famous youth, but for my truthfulness, vulnerable as it has made me to the most vile accusations.

You didn't hear? Lean closer.

Ah, I've got you then. Pray, don't squirm. Tender me this loose grasp of your thigh, and I'll give her to you as she gave herself to me.

Cinna stood just this close to me then. Three of us in the Santuarium Scholasticus. Always the configuration of three. Does it not bear contemplating? Cinna stood between myself and Mr. Doyle. Doyle kept his tremulous distance, his monocle suddenly a crazy metronome swinging from the flush of his neck. I could see that the eye from which it had so unexpectedly popped was afflicted with a garish twitch. I now realized the bulging glass had always kept it in check, more a prop for the open window than its enhanced transparency.

He almost stammered an utterance, but couldn't finally pry one lip free of the other's frozen grip.

"Help me," I plainly spoke to her. "Mr. Doyle has gone too far this time," and I moved toward the steel gurney across the room. This required a pirouette around the corner of my desk, a lifting of all my weight onto my toes to squeeze between the wall and the wood, and then a struggle to rein the centripetal force of the turning body back into the channel of a straightforward stride.

How humiliating that a fat man must resort to a dancer's contortion to navigate the narrow spaces of the most ordinary action, and so become the consummate parodist of his own handicap.

Had Cinna followed me across the room?

Yes. I could *hear* her breath idling beside me, as I prepared to lift the corner of the oilcloth that draped the entire length of the galvanized bier.

No. It was the weight of her thigh against my flank that let me *feel* her breathing. Because I remember that she held her breath to see what would be revealed. And so I also remember that in my mock-balletic haste to cross the room I had bounced Doyle out of the way and into a shrouded corner. The shadow cast by my desk lamp cut across his throat in a single stroke. The expression on his face might as well have been concealed in the executioner's cinched sack.

"This isn't me. Not my work. Not *me*," I protested to Cinna, with an unveiling flourish of one hand. You must know the gesture yourself, from your official duty to verify the victim's identity before grieving witnesses. In a single motion, I had laid bare the artful figurine that I mournfully envisioned would become the gargoyle of my professional disfigurement.

From his obscure corner of the room, Levant Doyle emitted a noise like the muffled click of a car door shutting on the hem of a gown, or a small hand. This was followed by a clattering to the floor of several gleaming implements that had been left in precarious balance upon the narrow ledge of the body tray, in the flustered moment of work's interruption. I could see the steel clarity of the situation in Cinna's recognition that these were not excavator's tools.

I looked toward the palsied gleam of the silver Medusa head and the near frantic tapping of Doyle's walking stick, which it crowned with such stationary will. I wished to solicit the spell that would turn us all to stone before Cinna could take another step.

Do you feel the stillness of the room in the stiffness of that posture which you've so graciously—I might even say lithely—acquiesced to? Lean closer. I have to whisper lower to hold the dioramic silence of the moment intact.

Ah, but the spell was broken. Cinna approached the gurney with her hands outstretched in a kind of ravenous supplication. They found their succor first in the stove chest cavity where the—I have to say manikin—seemed to have taken a fatal blow. The tips of Cinna's fingers already showed the dun stains of fixative emulsifier and yes, the adhesions of resinous glue.

The human frame was shattered in more ways than one, as whatever force had splintered the rib cage seemed to have loosened every jointed limb, giving the entire physique, if that is a proper term, the appearance of having been expertly boned. Only the cranium was limned with bone in a way that modeled features of a discernible face. It showed forth under Cinna's impatient fingers, as they were beginning to trace the lineaments of a visage that she suddenly realized she knew quite well. Doyle's self-portrait in mud. Doyle had peered deeply into a small hand mirror looking for just the right touch to model himself so well. This was his masterpiece.

Beyond the carefully distressed dermal veneer, so cannily solicitous of the microscope's severe scrutiny—the infinitesimal pockmarks of residual oxidation, the fibrous grain of the epidermis, and the uncannily fecal color and corpulence of the skin-shrunk muscle—there were revealed all of the familiar birthmarks. The vaguely squashed forehead. The strawberry nose. The fleshy lips that look like someone is always blowing through them. Least amusing of all was the faithful reproduction of the eye twitch as if a relentless camera had taken charge of the imitation of life when the mere hands of the forger became dulled to the minutiae of the work.

Cinna's own hands, clapped to her cheeks—her inspection of the outrageously imitated facial details had brought her close enough that she might have seemed to be puckering a kiss—began to tremble. Along with the pursed lips, the white-knuckled hands seemed to be battening back a torrent of speech, or tuning a bestial howl into a sirenlike alarm. For the rest of her body alerted itself into a near frenzy of speechless gesticulation. So manic was the upset that she abruptly gyrated into the corner of the room, shredding the curtain of shadow in which Doyle had successfully hidden his cowering presence from even my notice.

Her hands, which fastened upon his suspender straps—he must have shed the rubber apron onto the invisible floor—seemed, by that touch, to have uncaged her voice. It raised to a pitch I had never heard clamoring in her throat before now. And with each intensification of Cinna's vocalizing, Doyle became more of a frantic puppet on the strings of his own trouser support. The thick rope of her red hair, lifting and falling upon her powerful shoulders, seemed a self-flagellating incitement to do more violence to Doyle's limp person.

The words, if they were meant to be such, only tolled with a leaden weight. They resonated no sense. Only rang in the air like a buffeting breeze. Aeolian breaths to be imbibed with intoxicating delight. It was pure music to my ears.

Cinna's physical dexterity, which this Taste would have us think was exclusively known to him—I feel it in the musculature embossed on your forearm, buttressing your lean on the arms of this chair—proved her the master of the moment, beat by clarion beat.

Could there be better proof of love than an aria such as Cinna delivered on the collapsing stage of that ignominious afternoon? What more fervid devotion could she show than to set upon Doyle with the accusation that his handiwork would besmirch my reputation? And was that not the libretto to be gleaned, by anyone with a musical ear, from the noisy spectacle of her thrashing self, flown careeningly upon the prostrated Doyle? Don't the muscular tongues of those prima donnas who stalk the footlights, vocalizing in a language that deafens our understanding, nonetheless suffice to show us all of the emotions—euphoria, jealousy, rage, melancholy, loathing—by the mere swelling or raising of the pitch? And they show us love most diaphanously. In a soprano register the lover flutters up to our ears, as if they had lips.

Just so vividly did Cinna appear to be the lover out of the clanging tones that knelled against Doyle's battered head. She was my lover surely, as her voice climbed a new octave. What other emotion would have accounted for such a willingness to lose herself with such abandon, and at the same time, to grip the neck of this man so fiercely that he might never speak again, lest he garble my good name?

My arms opened to her with the warmest welcome, the most labile succor. My voice even heaved after a harmonics that might pacify her breast. And, by that feat, no doubt, I spared Doyle a crippling disability, beyond what his silver walking stick already ministered to, Medusa head and all.

In my unstinting embrace, Cinna's own grip upon my backbone was as fervent as it seemed to have been upon the uppermost vertebrae of Doyle's gristly neck.

You must pardon my insensitivity, holding you so tightly. Bound as I am to wring these memories from the pulp of here and now, no lesser grip will do. Since you say you want the truth, you might be solaced that such memories are as much flesh as blood, compared to what our livid friend here would testify. Possessed of a perfect memory, his version will nonetheless still only be a figment of feeling, nothing like the vibrant touch that you feel here and now, however embarrassing it might be for you to realize it.

Or are these arms about my shoulders more than just a bid to regain your balance, having leaned too far in solicitation of my testimonial, having lost your footing? Could it be that you hug me more than you hate me?

I remember perfectly how she looked in flight from the Santuarium Scholasticus. Red hair flying, a red mask that bled down her neck and into the opening of her shirt collar. And a look in the eyes that saw red in every direction. She seemed to peer in every direction, as if for a door more escapist than the one she'd just slammed in her wake.

What she didn't see apparently, was myself, twisting, reaching out, falling short of a shoulder. The swiftness with which she turned from me was a pulse of fevered breath on my startled face. I blinked and she was gone.

My mother's eyes. My mother's hair. These attachments were not breakable bonds.

All morning I followed Cinna like a rat in a maze, anticipating where she was by bumping my head against the blind alleys of my red-eyed intuitions. But, like the rat, I could not lift my head above the gray walls of my bafflement, to survey the gridded map of the find site from some imaginary *above*.

Find site. Yes, there is an irony in that term of our professional art, which seemed to put iron bars in front of my thinking about where she might be found.

I needed a car to drive as far as the next inhabited village. My hand slipped continuously on the steering wheel, a frightening mimicry of the snaky road, as if the wheel or the road were greased with the perspiration of my tightly clenched palms.

Luckily I stopped frequently along the twisting way, to check the sedge gullies on the side of the roadway, vividly mindful of the scenarios of foul play that are your own daily exercise, I'm sure.

When I parked before the village constabulary I was not seeking help, though in retrospect I probably should have appealed to the uniformed man perched at the high desk within. I should have appealed for some official surveillance, of what I was not yet in a position to know with certainty. Wouldn't I have seemed to be the crazy character then?

Instead I stood on the crumbling curb outside the constabulary and contemplated the narrow lane of the dreary hamlet. On days when there were reports from the find site that might merit a telephone communiqué, a few sodden newspapermen could be seen congregating here in the downpour. The village was our link to the world, a dark, lichen-skinned stone passageway to the bustle of modern times. Standing there in the commencing drizzle, I felt as though I might have been hewn from a block of peat myself, stooped and heavy browed, hideously scarred by the ancient rites, and beginning to come apart as the water gnaws the adhesive grain of my preservative.

My mother's eyes. My mother's hair. Wasn't I really foraging for them? Did I expect to find them in a brick alley, under the crookedly ajar lid of a foul smelling rubbish bin, like elements of an abandoned masquerade: black eye patch, false mustache, rubber nose, a double-hinged mouthful of stained and broken teeth, the red wig, the glass eyes of hazel hue? Didn't I believe that Cinna's mysterious whereabouts signified an almost characteristic abandonment of herself? I had known her willingness to lose herself in the callisthenic excesses of our limb-entangling passions. But always what she cast off accrued to my embrace of what I looked for in her eyes. Could she finally have decided to be herself?

A tea shoppe, a lemon-hued bulb winking above its half curtained window front, took tremulous shape in the greasy puddle that had formed surreptitiously at my feet. If I turned and took five easy steps I would surely find myself inside, dripping onto the stone tile floor, my hand finding its resting place on a wooden chair back, inhaling the vaguely algal steam from the teapots, like a sleepwalker whose dream world, in all its miniature detail, becomes a place he can stand up in, as he shuffles into wakefulness.

There I saw her. But it was not what I had looked for. It was she. But it was not Cinna's face. Sitting at a bare tabletop, not even imbibing, but staring at me as if she had waited a long time, she slowly smiled.

I recognized her by her outfit—the epauletted field shirt, the jodhpurs meekly unpouffed by the damp, the muddy boots laced to the knees—certainly not by the black Buster Brown wig or the green-rimmed sunglasses that blackened her eyes as well. That is how she disguised herself.

A test for me? A test of my passion for her? Was she standing now to show me I had passed a test? She was passing me. Would I go with her? Was she asking me to follow?

It was to a room in another building three doors down. Her steps seemed more trudging than mine, though I was the one in tow. We climbed a narrow flight of stairs at the back of a hallway that smelled so strongly of kerosene I feared the dampness in the carpeted steps made it little more than the long, shaggy fuse of an imminent combustion. Or shouldn't I say *conflagration*?

Conflagration had been a pet conceit, the one by which Cinna and I, in the flush of our affair, had flattered ourselves: that our passion would burn with more intensity than the loins of ordinary lovers. It was the torch we carried to one another in the subterranean passageways of doubt through which we traveled every day, from the public routines of work in the field to the secret recesses of our nightly rendezvous—where we incandesced.

No passageway could have been darker than the hallway at the top of those explosive stairs.

The light in the room was barely a candle glow, though a sizzle of tungsten kept up a noisy accompaniment to its faint illumination. In that flickering aura Cinna stood, soft focused, amid the crowding shadows, sepia toned, and except for the black wig and green-rimmed sunglasses, naked before me. I thought of a pornographic photo album passed over the shiny knees of gentlemen in stovepipe hats, a purloined daguerreotype embezzled by the loneliest of that taciturn crowd, for the enhancement of his most private fits of introspection.

Then this was certainly the test. The now off-kilter wig and glasses were challenges to my arousal before the familiar narrow hips and heavy breasts, and especially the undisguised pubic rouge, which Cinna should have known, the faintest light would have lit as flame.

Nothing passed between us then except the beating of butterfly wings that was my breath. But I knew she waited.

Perhaps Cinna imagined that the low light would better reveal what blows on the embers of my lustful heart. But my eyes would not adjust. I could see only the ludicrous disguise. And if the color of her pubic bush shone brazenly truthful in that light, and held the wig up to ridicule, the fact that I could not see her eyes nonetheless blinded me to the possibility of passion. My body felt clad in a chilly aspic. Movement would have aroused a gluey sensation in all my joints, the tackiness of flypaper, myself becoming the jet black and bug-eyed vermin nonchalantly folding and unfolding my useless wings, under the approaching scrutiny of a curious child.

I didn't move. And when I realized she was padding towards me—because her presence preceded the sound of her—I had no time to disguise my emotions, or to lash them down. I simply sobbed. I squalled. I moaned with all the mournful hawsers struggling to hold their little boats in port at storm tide. I blotted my eyes with embittered fists that I should have struck against my heaving breast in order to make the picture of pathos perfect. A perfect farce.

How much I realized the ludicrousness of the man whose passions are creatures of his mother's bedroom mirror. Such a man, should he find himself alone at last and sobbing for his losses, should he trudge home to that wishing well of sparkling reflections in his dead mother's bedroom, alas, would not even find the vaguest outline of himself in that nostalgic glare.

I saw myself at last for what I could not be to Cinna: a man who sees through the mirror glare, *here and now*. Surely if a birth was in the offing, it would be a bouncing baby boy. I, after all, was it.

I imagined that the blow Cinna landed on my cheek at that moment, sharp as broken glass, would scar, raising a jagged lightning bolt of livid tissue to remind me forever more of what I look like.

You see this fat man smile—even the corners of his mouth are bellied—as if my honesty should be to my discredit? Snickering, not sympathizing, as he would have us think. Isn't that evidence enough you cannot trust him? Think of him instead as a festering pillow of jizz. Bulbous, bleeding, prick-nose. Stinking clinker. Mountain of lice shite. Mongrelized fart cloud. Sanctimonious elephant stool. Smeggy-mouthed ear-shagger. Snuffling muff hound. Quim-faced arse picker. Flaming gob of minging sexjuice. Rat knacker. Filthy bog brush…

I have my book….

It could be in my book…

But do I remember this? It seems an omen. But it comes to me like the puzzle pieces of a shattered stone tablet. I believe this time Mr. Doyle has gone too far.

He leads his tours. "My museum," he yaps, in a more and more stentorian tone. The exhibit halls are always bellowing now. And he has begun to speak too freely of the specimens.

He declares he no longer has any need of the gold embossed ring binder of guide papers that our most earnest docents commit to memory before they embark upon these marble floors. It is not because he sports a good memory. Doyle says he is beginning to let the specimens speak for themselves. He says he is beginning to see that there is more to archeology than digging.

He *sees!*

Well, how unsighted must a person be, not to have spotted my raspberry-pitted rubber nose and droopy moustache, the barely graying full pate of hair—sprouting, in loose ringlets no less—the silver-tipped cane, that was a perfect imitation of the one he demurred to carry on these expeditions? A rough and readily improvised disguise was what I needed if I were to follow Dundeed's tour and be a reliable spy. My companions milling under the rotunda dome eyed me with perfectly appropriate suspicion. But Doyle even bumped into me, on the perimeter of the frenetic herding maneuver by which he was attempting to gather everyone into the first exhibition room. He hardly looked up from what had to be the uncanny coincidence of his sensing "a body without bones," as he had once dubbed my physique: having once softened his fist against my midriff in a playful sparring session between good naturedly competitive friends. Here we were again, testing one another.

The first room was uneventful. Doyle droned on for a foot-numbing time, having planted himself in front of the mural that illustrated the process of bog formation in six gradients of color. My tour brothers and sisters rubbed their eyes, yawned, punched themselves in the small of the back and prodded their reflections in the polished floor with the toes of their shoes.

Then Doyle conducted the forlorn troupe through an instructional hallway flanked by exhibit cases that were indiscriminately stocked with parts and accessories: a few stray limbs and appendages badly preserved, but mostly axe heads, leather belts, strips of woolen fabric, corroded knives, beaded necklaces, bone arrow points, a sheepskin cape. All of this Doyle whisked by with the haste of a distracted child, hastening the party of visitors after him, like the anxious parents, rushed onward by the mystery of where he might disappear to.

There was no mystery when we heard his voice beginning to inflate across the threshold of the first of the domed exhibit halls, an echo chamber for the magnitude of what was to be seen there. The glaring white circumference of the hall, made brittle as an eggshell with the morning light, was arrayed on its perimeter with minor table displays: specimens of crude artisanship, masks carved with the features of goat heads, wooden mallets, hempen bonds bearing decorative knots. But at the central point of the room, the axis of our rotation, the large glass exhibit case stood in full vertical proportion to the drama of earth and air it so viscerally displayed. ***DIRTMOUTH****, read the explanatory marquee.*

And yet I can't see it. For the moment, I can't see it. My memory, like the spade dropped in mid-stroke, impugns the strength of my writing hand, as though these fingers were prey to a palsy that does not afflict them. I can't see it.

But of course it was Doyle's voice that made the scene that day.

My feeble memory has a sure grip of that voice, which, after all, was not altogether his own, though its shrill tonality brings his mouth into a kind of livid focus. The purplish lips betrayed only the faintest tremors of the tongue, that seemed to lever its words from nowhere else but the throat of the female specimen shimmering behind the glass.

What puppetry, I had to confess! "I'm called Dirtmouth, I am..." The vocables themselves were even convincingly clotted with the black earth that so manifestly choked the specimen's eloquent orifice in her futile struggle to raise her head above it.

The visitor who approaches the exhibit case sees the peated surface of the death pit, reconstructed there in grain and particle with such dark authenticity that we can't believe when we stoop to it, that we are able to see below the surface too. The trussed and contorted pulse of the visible body, appearing so nakedly alive behind the clear window, made the girlish words choked out of thin air above our heads seem all the more alarming to the members of the group, who were now huddling around the exhibit in a circle that Doyle orbited with disturbing energy.

I have the spade well enough in hand to reveal how with his hands thrust deeply into his jacket pockets and snapping his knees high at every step, he marched with a forward tilt as if he were traversing a high-grown meadow, utterly distracted, a man alone with his thoughts in unbounded nature, while all the time the voice hovered over the exhibit case, occasionally slipping from its shrillest pitch to graver tones that almost dragged at Doyle's feet until, soon, it was soaring and swooping like a trapped bird bashing its wings against the invisible walls of a glass aviary.

She spoke with a convincing enough brogue, but, beyond the meek introduction, the only words that sounded a note of intelligibility seemed made up of the syllables of an altogether foreign tongue.

And so? And so?

Am I lost again so soon? Both of them left derelict and wandering in darkness now? Her birdlike voice. His demonical stride. Loosed from all worldly bearings by my unremembering hand. Can I save them with a knowing spurt from my pen? Or perhaps they can save me from this darkening stage upon which I stand so dizzily alone, where every next step could be a tumble into the pit. The orchestra pit, as it were. Sounds will abide, senses bristle without memory.

For the man without memory, things retain their substantiality but at the expense of the perceiver. The jumble of sensations is a horribly clanging affair. A cacophonous music stirs panic in the unremembering mind as it did under the deafening rotunda when Doyle commenced to quicken his orbit around our already stricken group, until he was launched into an unstoppable run, his hands beating the air above his head and shrieking in a voice that was unmistakably his own. It seemed to be choking him with its ferocity: "Listen! Listen! Listen!"

Had Levant Doyle expected, even hoped, that the voices of the by now tightly herded lambs that made up our company—all now heeling to my gravitational center—would begin to choir the piercing tones of their hysteria with his?

Which is how I suddenly remembered myself to myself. The chime of recognition sounded within me the knowledge that this, after all, was my condition. My malady. As if I had forgotten that even cacophonous music can be sung to.

And now I have the spade well balanced in my grip of the rolling pen point. At the core of that dinning chamber of echoes, I settled peacefully within myself. A voice there, orbiting my thought in some forgiving parody of Doyle's unforgivable behavior, soft and reserved, and without a trace of coercion, implored me to listen, listen, listen.

x x x x x

You're telling me that you have spoken with Mr. Doyle? While we were napping? And were we napping in your absence?

Then, from what you say, Mr. Doyle has finally taken a violent hand in things, for his own poor part. You can't wonder, can you?

But to take a silver Medusa's head to our founding exhibition case! Our foundling find! He casts the first stone with a vengeance doesn't he? It would almost be witty, if witticism were not such patent pathos in this case. Mr. Doyle's will to self-destruction is well known. I must say, I have never seen him lean with any real physical conviction on that walking stick. And in all our planning for the museum, we never considered the necessity for shatterproof glass.

No doubt he is already in your custody as well, and will be joining our glum circle momentarily, red faced, abashed, the brass-framed monocle remanded to the handkerchief pocket of the pin-striped jacket, the sealskin bowler pulled tightly over his eyes. He won't say a word, I assure you.

Or does the law merely countenance this as a private desecration of private property? His museum. Very well. Then we here will remain a lonely three.

It is quite true. The exhibit case is a controlled environment. It is a climate unto itself. Temperature. Humidity. Even atmospheric pressure. Brittle invariables of the glass world. Exposure to natural air would precipitate a catastrophic oxidation, even in a matter of minutes.

Then I agree. It is remarkable that the specimen, liberated from the shattered exhibition case, shows no sign of degradation by the elements.

A rarity. A rarity indeed. But aren't all the specimens, all, already rarities? If the word loudly declares a material scarcity, doesn't it silently admit a scarcity of knowledge as well? Like faces in a faded photograph, they stand at a blurred distance, beyond our powers of crystalline understanding. So why should the curiosity of this specimen's unique preservative nature be such a callisthenic conundrum for you? The specimen does not decay in air. So be it, I say. The beneficent creator and the black-hearted executioner say the same benediction. Should the archeologist, who is curator of both their handiwork, say any differently?

And what does Doyle know to do with the name Sophia Pasthand? It's nothing of his. Certainly not his to speak of. And I must say, it's very dirty-mouthed of him to make the allegation that the specimen in the shattered case, if she spoke at all, would want to speak to me.

If this is his allegation.

Is that his allegation?

× × × × ×

The one who loved her most must be her murderer, or the newspaper you laid beside me while I napped wouldn't have headlined it a *CRIME PASSIONELLE*. Then let me claim the privilege.

I will confess the crime. But I will not tender to the court any grisly details of the act, which, no doubt, you already possess in the lapidary files of your forensic record. Nor will I indulge your appetite for motive and the dreary theatrics of opportunity. No hand-wringing courtroom allocution to the step-by-step elements of the crime. These are your poor tools of excavation, which I fear would only risk further damage to the specimen.

I will tell you only that I am guilty, and that I welcome whatever punishment might be meted out that would be fully proportionate to my guilt. I'll willingly take my seat on the scales of justice. I promise you it will be a perfect balancing act. Imagine the violent lopsidedness were Dundeed to deposit his burden in the clanging balance pan.

Let Kraft Dundeed have his innocence. Is it not the saving grace of his malady, after all? If such malice can be mitigated by the ills of forgetfulness. Let Dundeed have his innocence. I'll have my passion.

And isn't passion the preferable sanctimony?

Innocence is a forger's game in any case. Look at him *here and now*. Even the obesity is for show. It shows his bloodiest strength for an eggshell fragility. Such bellies are voracious eaters. Then notice how unsavorily the hand that caresses it feigns the expectancy of the pregnant mother. And the arm he dangles that hand from is, in its thickness, the very figure of the cudgeling blow. And the shoulders. Their sag is no disguise for their breadth. I've seen him break a railroad tie across his back. The spring in the spine and in the knees—yes, and the calves of a dancer too!—is deceptively torqued. They say he's kicked a horse to death. The feet he seems to shuffle upon carry the inertia of lead weights. He is always looking for the softest parts of the body to land them. And is there any doubt that the fists that are rolled into the palms of those tallow hands are made to deliver the severest punishment to the face?

Let innocence be his! Then I'll kick his fuck in. The knobbing fanny tosser. Wanking bog plonker. Whinging prickwit. Ballocks confectioner. Bazz gardiner. Arse snogging bogtrotter. Gick sniffing geebag. Snake cooter. Mangy scutters trough…

I would have to spit to say any more.

EPILOGUE

Now I've heard enough.

Silence, I've learned, is like air that unseals the airless chamber. The breath of silence is the reagent of a chemical change affecting the loquaciousness it wafts upon. Just so, when the pores of the underground specimen breathe deeply enough from the lips of the first cut through the hermetic turf, it becomes a creature of oxidation. What was, now is. The difference is that, here and now, nothing remains the same. Nothing remains. That is the truth to be gleaned by silence.

In silence I have listened for you to listen to one another. And you have only talked. Talk is so self-preservative, don't you find it to be so? And yet I have learned some things from your talk.

Only the specimen that has not naturally mummified will not decay when exposed to air. It is fake, a titbit of Egyptian cleverness, a feeble artifice of the desperately living will, a crime against nature, a shrill curse word beating against the silence, as if it were a closed door.

The door, of course, is always open.

You have heard my silence, though it has discomfited you. It stirred tensions in your restive tongues. I know, it sets the teeth on edge. Nor has it been easy for me to endure the silence. Silence, after all, is a breather, between the bouts of speech which we are bound to resume, contenders that we are with one another. You have spoken. I fear you have spoken until you are breathless. I hear you clamoring for breath through the falling shovel loads of words that will bury you alive if you do not take a breather.

Now let me say something.